To Geeder Perry, eleven years old and free for the first time to make her summer on her uncle's farm something special, Zeely Tayber is the embodiment of dreams. Zeely tends the pigs that pasture on the Perry farm, but she is an extraordinary young woman to behold—especially to one as imaginative as Geeder. One day Geeder finds a photograph in an old magazine—a portrait of a Watutsi queen who looks just like Zeely. Suddenly she decides that the regal Zeely must be a queen too, and, swept up in her fantasies, she tells all the children in their little Ohio town.

Only Zeely herself can bring Geeder back to reality. How she succeeds is at once moving, surprising, and reassuring—to Geeder most of all.

VIRGINIA HAMILTON was born in Yellow Springs, Ohio. After many years in New York City she returned to Yellow Springs where she lives with her husband and children. Ms. Hamilton is the author of the National Book Award and Newbery Medal winner, *M.C. Higgins, the Great*, and the ALA Notables: *The House of Dies Drear*; *The Planet of Junior Brown* (also a Newbery Honor Book), available in Laurel-Leaf editions; and *The Time-Ago Tales of Jahdu.*

THE LAUREL-LEAF LIBRARY brings together under a single imprint outstanding works of fiction and nonfiction particularly suitable for young adult readers, both in and out of the classroom. The series is under the editorship of Charles F. Reasoner, Professor of Elementary Education, New York University.

ZEELY

by *Virginia Hamilton*

Published by
Dell Publishing Co., Inc.
1 Dag Hammarskjold Plaza
New York, New York 10017

Laurel-Leaf Library ® TM 766734, Dell Publishing Co., Inc.

ISBN: 0-440-99905-7

Reprinted by arrangement with Macmillan Publishing Co., Inc.
Printed in the United States of America
First Laurel-Leaf printing—May 1978
Second Laurel-Leaf printing—September 1978

*For Leigh Hamilton Adoff
and
Etta Belle Hamilton*

ZEELY

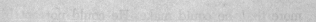

1

There was an awful racket and swoosh as the books John Perry carried slipped out of his arms and scattered over the floor.

"Wouldn't you know he'd do it? Wouldn't you just *know* it!" The voice of his sister, Elizabeth, echoed through the huge waiting room. Her mother shushed her.

"After all," said Mrs. Perry, "it's not so terrible to drop an armload of books. It could happen to anyone."

"But why does it happen to us?" Elizabeth cried. "And always when we're in a hurry to go somewhere!"

John Perry stood close to his father. He wanted to pick up his books, but the effort of running after them and bending down where they lay was more than he could make. He could not get his legs to move. Never had he been in a train-station waiting room. It was full of quiet people quietly going places. Now all of them stared at him. He lowered his head, trying to hide his face.

"No harm done, John," Mr. Perry said. "Next time, you needn't carry so many books." In a moment, he had gathered them up, giving half to Elizabeth to carry and half to John.

"No harm done!" Elizabeth whispered. "Goodness sakes, everyone in the whole place will think we're just little babies!"

"Elizabeth, stop that whispering," her mother said.

Elizabeth clapped her hand over her mouth. She didn't know she had spoken out loud to herself. She hadn't meant to. But she often talked to herself when she was nervous or upset. Like John, she'd never been in a train station. Before, her father and mother had driven them to the country. This time would be different.

"Aren't train stations just grand?" she said. "Look at those pillars—I bet they're all of three feet around. And the windows! Did you ever see anything so very high up?"

The windows were enormously wide and high. John Perry forgot his fear and lifted his head. He smiled up at the windows. Sunlight streaming down exposed sparkles of dust in a shaft to where they stood. Mr. and Mrs. Perry looked up, too. They all stood there, separated from the busy waiting room by the peaceful light and shadow.

It was Mrs. Perry who remembered there was a

train to catch. "Oh, my! Hurry, you two!" she said to John and Elizabeth.

Elizabeth fell in step beside her father, who had started toward the train platform. Mr. Perry carried both John's and Elizabeth's suitcases. He urged them along more quickly, for the gate to the train had opened. Most of the people had gotten aboard.

"Elizabeth, I want you to sit and act like a lady," said Elizabeth's mother.

Elizabeth did not look back to where Mrs. Perry walked with John. "Goodness," she said to herself, "do you think I don't know what's what? Leave me alone and I'll do what I'm supposed to do!"

Elizabeth heard her mother talking to John. "Remember to comb your hair," she was saying, "and don't bother people with questions."

"You can tell him not to open his mouth for the whole trip."

"Elizabeth," her father said, "calm down."

"Just tell him not to bother *me!*"

"Elizabeth!" her father said.

"Mind that you do whatever Elizabeth says . . ." It was Mrs. Perry talking to John.

Elizabeth heard her. She smiled and held her head up like a proper lady.

When Elizabeth first saw the train, she stopped. Mr. Perry shifted the luggage to one hand so he could take Elizabeth by the arm and lead her along. "I'm about to drop a suitcase," he said to her, "so you'd better hurry."

"Is that it?" Elizabeth said. "Is that the train?

How do we find our seats?" The train was quite long. Billows of steam rose from beneath the engine.

"I bet it weighs a ton!" said John, coming up behind Elizabeth. He walked around, looking at the engine. "I bet I could climb it," he said. "I bet I could make it go fast!"

Mrs. Perry hurried them aboard. Mr. Perry found their seats for them without any trouble. He put their suitcases in a rack overhead. When John and Elizabeth were seated, Mr. Perry stood a moment, looking down at them.

"Now remember," he said to Elizabeth, "after the midnight stop, the train will not stop again until morning. And the first stop of the morning, you and John gather your belongings and get off."

"Where do we get off?" Elizabeth asked. "Which is front and which is back?"

"Where's the bathroom?" asked John.

"Is there a water fountain?" asked Elizabeth.

"You can get off at either end," Mr. Perry said. "Where you find a door open and the conductor waiting, get off." Then, he showed them where the bathrooms and water fountain were.

Seated again in her seat, Elizabeth made her fingers dance on the window. "Do I have to tell anyone when I'm getting off?" she asked her father.

"Just get off at the first stop of the morning," Mr. Perry repeated. "You'll find Uncle Ross waiting for you there on the train platform."

There was little else to say. Mrs. Perry leaned

down and kissed Elizabeth and John. She told them to be good and to have a good time. They were to remember to obey Uncle Ross and not to play too hard. Mr. Perry kissed them and then looked carefully at Elizabeth.

"And now," he said to her, "I leave it all to you."

Elizabeth smiled at her father, tossed her head and looked as though she could take care of anything.

Mr. and Mrs. Perry hurried off the train. They had only a few seconds to wave at Elizabeth and John before the train pulled out of the station.

2

Elizabeth forgot all about sitting like a lady. She sat on her knees with her head pressed against the window. The glass cooled her hot face and hands and she was able to put her thoughts together.

"Well, the school term's over," she said. Her lips moved against the window but her voice made barely a sound. "We'll spend the whole summer on the farm with Uncle Ross. I ought to make up something special just because we've never ever gone alone like this!" She began figuring out what she might do that would be as important as travelling to the country without her father and mother.

John Perry leaned around Elizabeth to see out the window. He was terribly excited about making the trip but his manner was not as sure as his sister's. He was smaller than Elizabeth, but otherwise he was enough like her to be her twin. His eyes were black, like hers, and his skin, brown, with a faint red hue. He had a shock of dark, curly hair that tumbled over his forehead just as Elizabeth's did.

"You know what I'm going to do?" he said to Elizabeth. "I'm going to take off my shoes and socks. I don't see why I have to wait until we get to Uncle Ross' before I go barefoot."

"You'd better not," Elizabeth said. "I'll tell mother and you'll be sorry."

"You're the meanest girl I know!" John said. He sat back glumly in his seat.

Elizabeth wore short pants and a shirt for the train ride. There were seven strands of bright beads looped around her neck. She would have loved making the trip without John. She liked being by herself. Alone, she could *be* anybody at all and she would have only herself to take care of.

The train swept through a long tunnel. Elizabeth sat very still. She could feel John, rigid, beside her. "Are you scared, John?" she giggled. "Don't be afraid. It's just a mean, black, spooky tunnel!"

John held on tightly to the armrests of his seat. "I don't care for tunnels," he said. He had never been in a tunnel on a train and he did not like it at all.

By the time the train entered the open air again, Elizabeth had figured out what special thing would be as important as travelling alone to the country.

"I want you to listen," she told John. "From now on, you are to call yourself Toeboy—understand? No more John Perry, and not just for the train trip but for the whole summer." He was Toeboy, she told him, because at the farm he could go around without shoes all the time if he wanted to.

"I'm going to be Geeder," she said. "I am Miss Geeder Perry from this second on. Horses answer to 'Gee,' don't they? I bet I can call a mare to me even better than Uncle Ross!"

Toeboy whinnied and began to prance up and down, knocking into the pile of books stacked on the seat beside him. They clattered into the aisle. It took Geeder ten minutes to quiet her brother without raising her voice or hitting him.

"I could just give you a good smack, Toeboy!" she said. She was furious but didn't dare touch him. In the last few weeks, Toeboy had become fond of letter writing. He would whip out his note pad and scribble off something to her father if she so much as looked at him.

"Now, I'm not going to yell at you," she said, "because then people might stare. They'll think I'm not old enough to take care of you."

"You're not," Toeboy said. "I can take care of myself, thank you."

Geeder ignored him. She made a neat pile of the books on the floor in the space between the seats. The train rushed on as the last sunlight of the day slanted into rows of tall apartment buildings.

"Why do you get the window seat?" Toeboy asked, after a while. He was tired of leaning around Geeder to see.

"Because I've *got* it," Geeder said, "and I'm going to *keep* it."

Toeboy could tell by the tone of her voice that she meant what she said. He decided to read his books.

Geeder pressed her face against the window. She knew Toeboy was beside her and that their coach was fairly full of people. But she felt cut off from him, from the train, as if she were outside with the scenery.

"I never thought there could be so many buildings, with so many windows and people." Geeder's lips moved, making the slightest sound.

The train moved along an elevated track and she could see building after building for what seemed miles. The train went so fast she felt lonely for all the people left behind. Long streets looked like spokes of a wheel connected to nothing and going nowhere.

"What things happen to all these people?" Geeder whispered. "I don't suppose they all have farms to go to in the summer, like me and Toeboy."

That made her smile. Oh, it was nice that school was over so that she and Toeboy could leave. . . . It wasn't that she didn't like her home. She liked it well enough. You could go to the park or to a show. You could go for a drive in the car and have hamburgers and ice cream or you could play along the river. There was lots to do. But lately she'd grown tired doing things she had done time after time. It wasn't that she liked going to Uncle Ross' any better. The truth was that she didn't remember what it was like there.

"Let's see, there's the farm and the town, and there's Uncle Ross," she said to herself. But try as she might, she couldn't recall what she did at the farm three years ago. "Maybe I didn't do anything. Maybe I was just too young to do much."

This time, she promised herself, she would do everything and see everything and remember everything she saw.

"I won't be silly, either. I won't play silly games with silly girls."

Suddenly, her father's last words came back to her. At the same time, she saw that the tall buildings had given way to open country. There were houses and a few farms and fields. The train had gone beyond the river and she hadn't seen any of it. From then on, she set her mind on seeing everything. The waning day she saw as clear as morning in the country; her father's words, bright as sunlight in the fields.

"*And now, I leave it all to you,*" her father had said.

"Why, he means something will happen and I'm to take care of it!" she said.

Toeboy thought Geeder spoke to him. He'd been waiting for her to say something above a whisper so he would know she wasn't still angry with him.

"Geeder," he said, softly, "just look at this."

She ignored him.

"Geeder, it's something you'll never believe."

"Toeboy, you read your books and don't bother me."

"It says here," he began, "there are these people living way in the middle of Australia where there isn't any water. When they want a drink, they pick a big, fat frog and squeeze all the water out of it into their mouths."

Geeder gasped and spun around in her seat. "That's just awful!" she said, taking the book away from him to look it over.

"It doesn't hurt the frogs," Toeboy said. "They just go along until they fill up with water. Then, they get drunk up again."

Geeder tossed him the book. "Please don't bother me, Toeboy. I've too much to think about without worrying about you."

"What do you have to think about?" he asked.

"Oh, things," Geeder said, "things that happen."

"What things?" he asked.

"Never you mind, Toeboy," she said. "Be quiet and read your books."

Toeboy reached in his pocket for his note pad. Geeder saw him. She at once smiled pleasantly at her brother.

"Pretty soon, we'll go eat," she said, "and you can have ice cream and cake after you have dinner. Oh, we'll eat everything and then we'll come back here. They'll turn out the lights and you can sit by the window. You'll be able to see everything in the night—won't that be fun? Then, we'll go to sleep and before you know it, we'll be there and Uncle Ross will take us to the farm."

Toeboy forgot about writing to his father. The mention of food made his mouth water.

"Will the dining car be scary?" he asked.

"Not like the tunnel," she said. "Don't you worry. I'll take care of it."

3

The night ride passed quickly, as Geeder said it would. The trip had seemed almost too short. In the morning, Uncle Ross was there at the station to meet them. Geeder had nearly forgotten what he looked like. She had a picture of Uncle Ross in her wallet and a picture of him in her mind. The one in her mind was closer to what she saw waiting on the train platform: a big, powerful man, like her father, whose smile was broad and gentle.

Uncle Ross' eyes shone as he caught sight of them and he tipped his hat eagerly with a friendly swoop of his arm. As Geeder ran up to him, laughing, the suitcase banging against her leg, he held out an arm for her to hold on to.

"Well, look here!" he said. "Look what's come to stay!"

"I'm Toeboy!" Toeboy shouted, running up and

catching hold of Uncle Ross' free arm. "The train wasn't scary at all."

"And I'm Geeder," said Geeder. "You must remember because we'll be Geeder and Toeboy for the whole summer on the farm."

"Geeder, is it?" Uncle Ross said, "and Toeboy. New names for a new summer. I like that! Give me a chance to catch my breath and I won't forget those names, ever!"

Uncle Ross hurried them into his battered old truck. Geeder recalled that it smelled always of leather and cigars.

At the farm, Geeder saw everything for what seemed the first time. She went in and out of the rooms, looking over all the antique furniture and fixtures Uncle Ross had collected at auctions over many years.

Uncle Ross and Toeboy walked behind her. "I'd hate to think you'd forgotten what my house looked like inside," Uncle Ross said, teasing her.

Geeder stood fingering a faded piece of silk folded neatly on an old end table. "It's not that I don't remember," she said. "I guess it never mattered before whether I remembered or not."

"But it matters now?" Uncle Ross asked.

"Oh, yes," Geeder said. She felt a sudden, sweet surge of joy inside. "Everything matters now!"

"Why?" asked Toeboy.

"Just never you mind," she said to him. "But I'll tell you this much. I'm three years older than the last time I was here. That means I know ten times as much as I did then."

Uncle Ross smiled, noting the great change in the children. He said nothing about it, however. He left them so they could roam the house on their own. "Well, call me if you find anything you don't know about," he said to them as he left.

There was a pantry in Uncle Ross' house. Toeboy and Geeder hung on to the door and looked inside carefully.

"I don't remember this at all," Toeboy said.

"Well, I do," Geeder said. "I don't remember it being so large, though, with so much food."

They couldn't decide if the pantry had been there the last time they visited the farm, so they called Uncle Ross. When he came, he told them the pantry had been just where they found it since the house was built.

"There's not another house in these parts with a pantry this size," he told them. He stood rocking on his heels in the center of the room, smiling proudly. "Each year, I put up beans, tomatoes, applesauce and jelly, among other things. Oh, I don't use half of it in a year," he said, "but I like giving it to folks in the village. These days, not many people put up food the way I was taught to."

The pantry was a large square. On every side were cupboards full of canned goods up to the ceiling. Geeder walked to the center of the room and slowly turned around until she had every cupboard fixed in her mind.

"Isn't it just the nicest place?" she said. "I love it, with all the jars and big cupboards."

Uncle Ross laughed. "Well, then, you can come

in every day and pick out all the food we'll need for each meal. That way, you'll get to know this pantry as well as I do and it will get to know you."

Toeboy wasn't much interested in the canned goods or the cupboards, even if they did reach clear up to the ceiling. But he did want to stand in his bare feet on the cement floor. He took off his shoes and socks hastily, and stood there. The coolness curled his toes.

"I think I'll just sit on the floor," Geeder said. She sat down with her back against the wall. She felt comfortable and decided she would sit on the floor for five or ten minutes each day.

Off the pantry there was a pump room.

"What in the world kind of place is this?" asked Toeboy.

"Uncle Ross—Uncle Ross!" Geeder called. He had left so that they could explore again. "Look, come and see this *place!*"

Uncle Ross came in a hurry, wondering what discovery the children had made in his old, familiar house. Then he saw it was the pump room. It was his favorite place of all.

"Now, you've come to something!" Uncle Ross said. "It's been thirty years since a house was built with one of these rooms."

"What in the world do you use it for?" Toeboy asked.

"Maybe you won't want to use it for anything," Uncle Ross said, "but I come in here when I need a drink of water that's finer than any other."

The pump room was quite a small place with just a hand pump attached to a square tub.

"Before there was running water in houses," Uncle Ross said, "people had pump rooms. There, they filled buckets with icecold well water for drinking and for heating on the top of wood-burning stoves."

Toeboy went up to the pump and cautiously pumped the handle a few times. There wasn't even a trickle of water.

"The pump has to be primed," Uncle Ross said to Toeboy. "Go get a pitcher from the dining room and fill it with water from the tap in the kitchen."

When Toeboy came back with the full pitcher, Uncle Ross showed him how to pour it slowly into the opening around the plunger.

"Now. You pump the handle," he said to Geeder.

Geeder pumped. Soon, they heard a dry, harsh sound. A minute later, water came gushing out.

"Have a drink," Uncle Ross said. He took a tin cup from a hook by the door and filled it, first offering it to Geeder and then to Toeboy.

"Oh!" Geeder said. "That's just the sweetest water!"

From that moment on, they refused to drink the perfectly good water from the sink in the kitchen and feasted in the pump room on well water cold as ice.

The rest of the house was large and spread out. Geeder supposed all farmhouses were like that.

Her favorite place was the parlor; it was silent, with blinds and curtains drawn to keep out the heat.

Standing in the room, she didn't know she had begun to talk to herself. "Look at all those old pictures," she said. Photographs, yellow with age, lined the walls and the tops of tables. "I'll bet that one is Uncle Ross when he was a boy. And that one is him for sure as a young man. I don't even have a memory of those other people. Probably Uncle Ross doesn't either, the pictures are so old."

There was a large photograph of a woman she knew to be Uncle Ross' wife, Aunt Leah. She was no longer living.

"She's awfully pretty," Geeder whispered. "I wish I could have known her."

The parlor had comfortable chairs, a sofa with many soft pillows and tables with drawers full of candy. Some of the candy tasted as though it had lain in the drawers for years, but Geeder ate it anyway. There was an upright piano against the far wall, away from the windows.

"I think I'll just play it once," Geeder said. She sat down on the piano bench and touched the keys gently. The sound came forth muted, as if it had waited a long time. The soft tone thrilled her.

"I can play a few songs a little bit." She spoke more to the piano than to herself. "I wish I could play well. I wish I knew a lot of pretty songs that would just fill up this room!"

A breeze pulled the blinds in and out against the window screens. The lace curtains were sucked up and down along the blinds, making a queer sound all of a sudden. Geeder felt a chill creep up her neck. The photographs seemed to look through her, as though she were a stranger.

She got up and, not looking back, flounced out of the room. "There's nothing you can *do* with an old piano," she said.

She wandered into the hall, where there was a cherry-wood staircase. She had noticed it when she first came into the house. Uncle Ross had said it was new, that the old one had fallen down in a heap a long time ago. It led, curving gently around, to the bedrooms above. The stairs had been in the back of her mind ever since she sat down at the piano. And the banister was the kind of thing she could touch and know.

"Better than old, yellowed photographs anytime," she said. She tried sniffing the banister. "It smells just like the tallest tree in the woods!"

Upstairs, she and Toeboy had separate bedrooms on opposite sides of a long corridor. Her room had a large, soft bed, a bureau with a mirror that she could turn any way she wished and two antique cherrywood chairs with silk cushions. She opened her suitcase and put all her clothes away in the closet and bureau. At the bottom of the suitcase was a box full of the rest of her necklaces. These she hung from the bedposts and the backs of the chairs. When she lay on the bed, the necklaces made her feel that she rested among stars.

Across the room from the bed were windows

that looked out on the rear yard, a big, empty barn and a smaller shed.

Since he no longer farmed, Uncle Ross kept no livestock about. There was just a fenced-in yard at the side of the house for the chickens.

Soon, Geeder got up from the bed and left her room. Slowly, she went over the whole house. Uncle Ross was somewhere outside, and she supposed Toeboy was with him. She had no one to bother her and could take her time. She went to Toeboy's room. His bed was large like hers and his windows looked out over the front yard and the high hedge that shielded the house from the road. She put all Toeboy's clothes away and stacked his books neatly on the floor by the bed.

"We'll have to get a bookcase for all these books," she said, "or he'll have them scattered from one end of the house to the other."

She went to Uncle Ross' room. "I don't suppose he'd mind if I just look in," she said. "I won't touch anything." She crept inside, careful not to make a sound, nor to bump against any furniture. Uncle Ross' room was much larger than hers and Toeboy's. He had a long, wide desk by the windows. There were many photographs on it, too. Geeder was pleased to find a picture of herself and Toeboy. "Now when was that taken—and who took it?" She couldn't recall posing for the picture. But she noticed at once that she and Toeboy were no bigger than babies. "Oh, the last time we were here," she whispered, "when we played silly games!"

Geeder walked around Uncle Ross' room several times, taking in everything she saw. All around her was a faint scent of sachet. It smelled the same as the photographs on Uncle Ross' desk looked—old, dry, clouded and dusty.

"I smell cigars, too," she whispered, "and soap and—my goodness—hay!"

Geeder stood still in the room, then slowly backed out of it. A chill crept up her neck.

"Oh," she said. "Old things. Waiting for something new to happen."

She walked slowly down the winding staircase, gently holding on to the cherrywood banister. Downstairs, she stopped in the pump room for a drink of water. When she had finished, she sighed with satisfaction and went quickly outside.

Sunlight hit her full in the face. Heat, with the scent of grass, blew in her nostrils. "Toeboy! Where are you? It's hot as blazes!"

She found Toeboy digging in the rich, black soil by the barn. He had found a squirming colony of earthworms. "Here, let me attach them," Geeder said. She tied the worms together, carefully, so as not to harm them. The worms wiggled. She and Toeboy laughed.

"They'll make a nice octopus for Uncle Ross' pond," Toeboy said.

"The pond!" Geeder had not remembered it. "Toeboy, let's get going!"

The pond was far back on Uncle Ross' land, in a pie-shaped section behind his west field. The section had never been much good for farming. Sycamore trees grew at random in it, and in the middle of these was the pond. It was not a deep pond, but it was good for wading up to the waist. They took off their clothes and waded in, heedless of the cold. When they had had enough, they put on their clothes again and sat dangling their feet in the water.

Geeder looked out through the trees, listening to sounds of trucks on the road which passed the house. She could even hear people talking a long way off. She imagined she heard what went on in town—people shopping and saying hello. It was then that she thought to rename the town.

"I'll call it Crystal," she said to Toeboy. "If you stand on the road, you can probably see the beginning, the middle and the end of it, just the way you can see through a piece of glass."

Geeder thought about the road. It curved for a mile through Crystal and then wound away from the town around a forest of catalpa trees to Uncle Ross' farm.

"Leadback Road! That's what I'll call it," she said. "Because where does it lead to?"

"Here!" Toeboy said.

"That's right!" Geeder said. "Crystal has a crack in it, Toeboy, and the crack is Leadback Road!"

4

The first day at the farm, Geeder and Toeboy looked over the hogs in Uncle Ross' west field. These were no ordinary animals, but prize razorback hogs owned by a Mr. Nat Tayber and his daughter, who rented the land from Uncle Ross.

"Look at the size of those hogs!" Toeboy said.

"They're big, all right," Geeder said, "and they're mean. I wouldn't get too close to them even if I had to."

They leaned on the fence, looking in at the hogs. The hogs wallowed around, eating and rooting in the earth with their snouts. Often they came close to the fence but veered away as they caught the scent of Geeder and Toeboy.

"Let's go," said Geeder. "I don't believe they like us here."

They fed a bit of corn to Uncle Ross' two

hundred leghorn chickens. They could feed them as much corn as they liked, Uncle Ross had said. And they could gather up eggs whenever they had a mind to.

"Well, it's the truth. I can do whatever I want," Geeder said to herself. Still, not one thing had taken place that fit with her father's words "*And now, I leave it all to you.*"

That was why, when evening came, Geeder decided to spread sheets and blankets out on the front lawn. She and Toeboy would sleep outside and maybe they would see a comet.

Toeboy liked looking up into the sky, as long as Geeder was talking. The sound of her voice made the night less strange and he felt safe. He had made his bed partly beneath a sprawling lilac bush close to the house. Geeder had made hers near the high hedge that shielded the house from the road. Toeboy felt so good that he decided to get up and make his bed next to Geeder's.

"I think I'll come over there," he called to her.

"Better not," she said. "Just better stay where you are."

"But I want to sleep by the hedge, too," he said.

"I know one thing," Geeder said. "Late at night in the country, night travellers walk along dark roads."

"What?"

"Night travellers," Geeder said again, "and they usually come up when you're just about asleep."

"What kind of things are they?" asked Toeboy.

He dug his legs deeper among the branches of the lilac bush.

"I'll tell you this," Geeder said. "If you see one, you'd better close your eyes fast and dive as far under the covers as you can go. They don't like kids watching them. In fact, they don't like anybody watching them!"

Toeboy stayed uneasily beneath the lilac bush. He was glad to be so near the house, for if he heard any sound, he could race inside. He did not mind at all seeing half stars and a half-moon through the lilac leaves.

Geeder turned around to see what Toeboy was doing and saw that he had pulled most of his bedding all the way under the lilac shrub. That nearly made her laugh out loud. She had made up the whole thing about the night travellers. She was only trying to frighten Toeboy—not for any really mean reason, but just because he was little and was easy to scare. As far as she knew, nobody walked late at night along this dark road.

But maybe ghosts do, she thought. A chill passed up her spine and she closed her eyes tight for an instant to make it go away.

"Toeboy," she called, "are you still awake?"

"I'm awake," he said. "I don't want to sleep yet." He lay fingering the cool leaves of the lilac.

"Then I'll tell you all about stars," said Geeder, "since you're so wide awake."

Geeder talked about the stars and the night. She knew Toeboy had gone to sleep when he no longer asked her anything or chuckled about what she said.

A long time passed. Geeder dozed and awoke with a start. The grass beyond the tip of her toes was wet with dew. She pulled the blankets more tightly around her, tucking her feet safely inside. She had closed her eyes again when she heard a rustling sound on Leadback Road.

Some old animal, she thought. The sound grew louder and she could not think what it was. Suddenly, what she had told Toeboy flashed through her mind.

Night travellers! She dove under the covers.

But something's happening! she told herself, poking her head out again.

It took all her courage to crawl out of the covers and the few feet over the wet grass up to the hedge. She trembled with fear but peeked through the hedge in spite of it. What she saw made her bend low, hugging the ground for protection. Truthfully, she wasn't sure of what she saw. The branches of the hedge didn't allow much of a view.

Something tall and white was moving down the road. It didn't quite touch the ground. Geeder could hear no sound of footsteps. She couldn't see its head or arms. Beside it and moving with it was something that squeaked ominously. The white, very long figure made a rustling sound when she held her breath. It passed by toward town.

Geeder watched, moving her head ever so slowly until she could no longer see it. After waiting for what seemed hours, quaking at each sound and murmur of the night, she crept back to bed, pulling the covers over her eyes. She lay, cold and scared, unable to think and afraid even to clear her dry throat. This way, she fell asleep. She awoke in the morning, refreshed but stiff in every muscle.

5

Geeder lay for a moment, watching mist rise from the pink, sweet clover that sprinkled the lawn. The air smelled clean and fresh and was not yet hot from the sun.

"I've got to decide," she whispered. In the stillness, the sound of her own voice startled her. She turned carefully around to see if Toeboy had stirred. The tangled bedding deep in the lilac bush did not move.

"If I tell Toeboy about the night traveller," she whispered, "he might not want to sleep outside any more. Just think of it! Not more than a few hours ago, an awful, spooky thing walked by here!"

Geeder wasn't at all sure she wanted to sleep outside again, herself.

"Goodness knows what a night traveller will do

if it sees you watching! Maybe I'd better tell Uncle Ross. . . . Maybe I shouldn't."

Geeder knew it would take her a while to figure out what course to take. Almost any minute now, the people Uncle Ross rented land to would come down the road. Uncle Ross had said they came every morning as soon as the sun was well up in the sky. It was just about time, and watching them would be something to do.

When her dew-soaked blankets grew warm from the sun, Geeder whistled for Toeboy as softly as she could. Turning around, she saw one eye peek out from the lilac bush.

"Wake up, Toeboy!" she whispered loudly. "I think I hear them coming!"

Toeboy leaped up before he looked where he was going and hit his head against a branch. Leaves spilled dew all over him. He was wet and still half asleep when Geeder yanked him to the ground before they could be seen.

They knelt low by the hedge. Trying not to move or blink an eye, they watched Mr. Tayber and his daughter come into view along Leadback Road. What they saw was no ordinary sight. They watched, spellbound, for nothing in the world could have prepared them for the sight of Miss Zeely Tayber.

Zeely Tayber was more than six and a half feet tall, thin and deeply dark as a pole of Ceylon ebony. She wore a long smock that reached to her ankles. Her arms, hands and feet were bare, and her thin, oblong head didn't seem to fit quite right on her shoulders.

She had very high cheekbones and her eyes seemed to turn inward on themselves. Geeder couldn't say what expression she saw on Zeely's face. She knew only that it was calm, that it had pride in it, and that the face was the most beautiful she had ever seen.

Zeely's long fingers looked exactly like bean pods left a long time in the sun.

Geeder wanted to make sure Toeboy noticed Zeely's hands but the Taybers were too close, and she was afraid they would hear her.

Mr. Tayber and Zeely carried feed pails, which made a grating sound. It was the only sound on the road besides that of Mr. Tayber's heavy footsteps. Zeely made no sound at all.

You would think she would, thought Geeder, she was so long and tall.

Geeder and Toeboy stayed quiet as the Taybers passed, and the Taybers gave no sign that they saw them hiding there. Uncle Ross had said that they were not known to speak much, even to one another. They had not lived in Crystal always, as Uncle Ross had.

Geeder and Toeboy watched the Taybers until they went out of sight. It was then that Toeboy said, "Let's go watch them in the field."

"No," said Geeder quietly, "no, Toeboy." She could not possibly have made him understand how stunned she had been at seeing Miss Zeely

Tayber for the first time. Never in her life had she
seen anyone quite like her.

Later on, as they fed the chickens, Geeder
talked to Toeboy about the arrival of the Taybers
in Crystal.

"They must have come early one morning," she
told him. "They might have come from the west
but I suspect they came from Tallahassee. They
brought all their wild animals with them in a
wagon train and they bought that house they live
in from Mr. Crawley."

"How could they come in a wagon train?" Toeboy wanted to know. Geeder was thinking and
didn't answer him.

"Mr. Tayber came down the road to see about
using some of the west field," Geeder said. "Uncle
Ross was to get a third of the profit from the sale
of the best razorback hogs."

"But why would Uncle Ross rent land to strangers?" Toeboy asked. "And what is 'a third of the
profit'?"

"Oh, goodness, Toeboy!" Geeder said. "I don't
know what 'a third of the profit' would be. And if
Uncle Ross waited until he got to know the Taybers the way you know ordinary people, he'd wait
forever. Listen." She stood very close to Toeboy,
as though the chickens might hear and she didn't
want them to. "All of Crystal knows only a few
things about the Taybers."

"What things?" Toeboy asked.

"Well, they know that Zeely Tayber is awfully
tall for a girl. Even Nat Tayber is very tall,"

Geeder said, "but not too tall for a grown man."

"What else do they know?" asked Toeboy.

"The Taybers like to be left alone," Geeder said, counting off on her fingers. "Zeely's mother is dead. Both Nat and Zeely have thin noses and very high cheekbones."

"Maybe the Taybers are Indians," Toeboy said.

Geeder had to laugh. "The Taybers are colored people," she said, "just like you and me and Uncle Ross. But they are different from any people I've ever seen. We don't know what kind of person Zeely is." Geeder's voice was full of the awe she felt for her. "But you know what I think? I think we've found a new people that nobody's ever heard of!"

All that morning, Geeder talked to Toeboy about Zeely. When they sat down for lunch with Uncle Ross, Toeboy was surprised by the off-handed way Geeder asked, "How long have those Tayber people been around this town?"

"Oh, it's been about a year and a half now," Uncle Ross said.

"That's a long time," Geeder said. "I guess you've gotten to know Mr. Tayber and his girl real well in all that time."

Uncle Ross smiled. "No," he said, "I wouldn't say that. The Taybers aren't easy to know, although they are speaking-polite to most folks."

"What would you say then?" asked Toeboy.

"What would I say when?" Uncle Ross replied.

Geeder wished Toeboy would just keep quiet. "He means to say that if you don't know them well, then what way *do* you know them?" she asked. "And why don't you know them well when they're in the west field every day working over those animals?"

Uncle Ross took a careful look at Toeboy and a much longer look at Geeder.

"Toeboy means to say all that?" he said to Geeder. "Well, I mean to say just what I did say. Mr. Tayber and his daughter live to themselves. They stay aloof from the whole town." He paused. "One day, the town had no thought of them. The next day, there they were, hammering and putting storm windows in that old house once owned by Jacob Crawley."

"Just like that?" Geeder said, snapping her fingers.

"No, not exactly like that," Uncle Ross said. "Now that I think about it, there had been time . . . room . . . for people like them among us. It's like it took them a long time to get here. The first time we see them, they are taking care to fix up that house. Strangers. And they stay on taking their time, still strangers. That's all right, the way I see it."

"Strangers," Geeder said. But that was all she said. She asked no more questions.

But by nightfall, Geeder was ready to talk about Zeely Tayber once more. As she and Toeboy lay in their beds on the lawn, she began.

"You would think a lady like Zeely would have all kinds of friends," Geeder said. "I mean, being so tall and being so pretty. But there she goes with just old Mr. Tayber. She hardly even talks to *him.*"

"He doesn't talk much to her, either," Toeboy said.

"That's because both Zeely and Mr. Tayber are different," Geeder said, "with ways about them none of us can understand."

Toeboy lay beneath the lilac bush, hugging the covers around himself. He listened to the rise and fall of Geeder's voice and was lulled into a deep sleep.

Geeder stopped talking. She was watching the stars when there grew in her mind a lovely picture. . . . It was daytime, with sunlight spilling over Uncle Ross' farm. She sat in shade on a grassy slope beside Leadback Road. Miss Zeely Tayber came gliding down the road. Her face and arms were shiny from heat and walking so long in the sun. She came right up to Geeder. She had been looking for her.

"Geeder, have you waited long?" Miss Zeely said. "I would dearly love a drink of water from the pump room."

Geeder brought Miss Zeely a drink of water in a tall glass, and a silk handkerchief. Miss Zeely sat beside Geeder, sipping the water. She wiped her face with the handkerchief and then dried her hands. When she had finished, she folded the hanky and placed it in Geeder's palm.

"Geeder Perry," said Miss Zeely, *"I don't know what I would do without you."*

Geeder pretended she hadn't done anything at all. . . .

"Miss Zeely Tayber," she whispered to the stars, "oh, Miss Zeely!"

Her hand touched something cool and heavy beside her. Uncle Ross' flashlight! She had taken it from his workroom. She meant to shine the light on the night traveller just as it passed by the house.

Suddenly alert and watchful, she listened to the silence around her.

"If the night traveller tries to bother me, I'll throw the flashlight at it," she muttered. "And if that doesn't stop it, I'll scream and wake up the whole town!"

But Geeder was tricked by the fresh night air into falling asleep. Many times she roused herself but did not awaken. Once she said in her sleep, "Is that you? Is that you coming?" It seemed that a voice came through the hedge, murmuring, "Yes, child, now sleep." It was her mother's voice. She slept more calmly then. She dreamed of home and people she knew there. In the morning, she was mad as a bull at having fallen asleep and had no recollection of the dream.

6

As the weeks passed, fine and sluggish, Geeder and Toeboy fell into a lazy routine. Each morning, they arose early to watch the Taybers come down Leadback Road. Each night, they talked of Zeely Tayber under the stars. Yet, try as she might, Geeder couldn't learn anything new about Miss Zeely. She feared all that was to happen had already taken place.

Some of the village children got into the habit of stopping by the farm to see if Geeder and Toeboy wanted to play. Toeboy either went off with them or invited them to wade in Uncle Ross' pond. When the children stayed at the farm, Geeder hid in the sycamores.

"I can't think straight about Zeely with them around," she said to herself. She didn't want anyone other than Toeboy to know about Zeely until she, herself, knew more. Many times, she had to take Toeboy aside to warn him never to mention Zeely to the others.

"I don't see why," Toeboy said.

"Toeboy, if you do, I'll never ever talk to you again!"

When Toeboy ran off to town with the children, Geeder waded and floated in the pond. She tried to outdistance the water striders, but the long legs of the striders fairly skimmed over the pond. Often she dug in the earth, looking for insects. She found a host of maggots feasting on an apple core. She didn't know they were the larvae of flies until Uncle Ross told her.

"All life changes," Uncle Ross said. "Some eggs change into chickens, some worms into butterflies."

The way Uncle Ross said what he did made Geeder feel stranger inside.

"It's too hot here," she said. "I think I'll just get away for a while." She slipped off to a nearby farm where there were fields of wheat and corn.

Geeder sat down in the middle of a long corn row. She pulled weeds to chew on. Purple morning glories twined up the cornstalks. Their scent mixed with that of the cornsilk and the black soil.

"It's awfully quiet here," she said. She didn't know why, but she felt kind of lonely.

"Everything is just dull. Nothing's any fun any more."

She stayed hidden in the corn until the odor of

the morning glories brought yellow jackets on the
back of the heat.

Geeder went to the wheat fields. The wheat
closed in behind her as she crept through it. The
slightest breeze caused the wheat to whisper and
bow.

"It talks to itself," she said, "just the way I do."
She made a nest by bending the wheat to the
ground. She lay on it, listening. She was cooler
here. The wheat was still green, keeping its mois-
ture.

"I bet Miss Zeely Tayber is lying down somewhere, resting like I am. I bet she doesn't have a
soul to talk to, either."

Geeder closed her eyes and folded her arms beneath her head. In no time at all, Miss Zeely Tayber came walking out from the dark of her
thoughts. . . . She and Miss Zeely locked arms
and ran to the other side of the wheat field, where
Miss Zeely lived in a great stone house. There was
a swimming pond hidden by plots of corn cockles
and bluebells. She and Miss Zeely stayed forever
just swimming and taking their ease of the sun. No
one could find them. . . .

Geeder slept through the hottest part of the
day, waking only when the sun slid off westward.
Her mouth was dry; she was chilled from the
damp earth. She did not feel at all rested.

"What's the matter with me?" she asked herself.
"What's wrong with everything?"

When she returned to Uncle Ross' farm, she
found that supper was ready. She ate little and

talked hardly at all. Uncle Ross glanced at her often but said nothing about the odd way she was
acting. Instead, he told her and Toeboy something
that took them by surprise.

"Nat Tayber plans to move forty of his prize razorback hogs tomorrow morning," he said.

"Move them where?" asked Toeboy.

"All the way down the road," Uncle Ross said,
"through town and then out to Red Barn."

"What's Red Barn?" asked Geeder, her voice
barely above a whisper.

"Why, I know you've seen it," Uncle Ross said.
"You must have passed it coming in on the train.
It used to be a farm but now it's a clearing house
for livestock. It's about a mile and a half from
here, a big place."

"And Mr. Tayber is going to move hogs all that
way?" asked Toeboy.

"Yes, to have them weighed and sold," Uncle
Ross said.

"I bet Miss Zeely is going to help him!" Geeder
said.

"I expect she will," Uncle Ross said.

Geeder kept her eyes on her plate, and forced
herself to eat.

I want to be sure and see Miss Zeely, she
thought. Maybe she'll ask Uncle Ross if I can help
her with the sows. If she'll ask him, I'll be able to
walk right beside her all the way into town—
maybe clear to Red Barn!

7

When the morning came, Geeder and Toeboy had the long, boring task of feeding Uncle Ross' two hundred leghorns.

"Any other day, I wouldn't mind," Geeder grumbled, "but if we're to see old Nat move his hogs, we'll have to hurry." At seven o'clock, she sent Toeboy off to fib to Uncle Ross.

"Geeder and I don't want any breakfast," Toeboy said. "We're not hungry at all." He was starving but he tried not to show it as Uncle Ross stared at him hard. Toeboy promised himself that later he would tell Uncle Ross the truth.

"You and Geeder be early for lunch then," Uncle Ross said.

Toeboy said they would and ran back to the chicken yard in search of Geeder.

Geeder was busily throwing great arcs of

chipped corn in every direction. She loved the
way it glinted golden bright in the sun. It was
Toeboy's job to empty the water pans and troughs
and refill them with fresh water.

"Why don't you watch where you throw the
feed?" he yelled at Geeder. He had to stop his
work to brush corn from his hair. A lot of feed fell
on top of the chicken coop, where the roosters
would find it eventually.

"Just stay out of my way," Geeder said. "I've
got to feed these chickens, don't I?"

They weren't half through with the chickens
when a terrible, throbbing squeal pierced the air.
Birds in the Chinese elm trees, bobwhites and
bluejays, set up a furious chatter, then flew away.
Geeder dropped her feed pail and started running.
She had reached the gate of the hen yard when
her good sense told her to stop. She rushed back
to the chickens, stumbling and groping for the
feed pail.

"Something awful has happened," she said.
"Hurry up, chickens, I've got to go help Miss
Zeely!"

By the time she and Toeboy reached the west
field, Nat Tayber and Uncle Ross stood over a
young sow.

"She's caught her hindquarter in the fence,"
Uncle Ross said. The lower shank of the sow's left
leg was torn and bleeding through mud-matted
hair. She quivered over her whole body and
snapped and squealed as Nat Tayber ran his finger over the wound.

Zeely Tayber was there, standing at a distance, shucking corn into pails. She stood tall and straight, with a long shadow of herself thrown by the sun toward the animals.

"She acts like nothing has happened," Geeder whispered to herself.

Zeely stood absolutely still except for the movement of her hands.

Geeder tried whistling, but if Zeely Tayber heard her, she gave no sign. Once, Zeely paused to look in the direction of the injured sow. Then, as before, she went on with her work and was silent.

Nat Tayber and Uncle Ross stared at the bleeding sow.

"We'd better get her to your barn," Nat Tayber said.

"We'll have to lift her," Uncle Ross said, "and that's not going to be easy."

Nat Tayber found some twine and tied the sow's legs together. That done, he and Uncle Ross lifted the sow gently and, struggling, carried her to the barn.

Geeder and Toeboy stayed by the hog pen.

"Geeder, let's go," Toeboy said. "This place smells awful!"

"I don't care if it does," Geeder said. "I want to see what Zeely's going to do. You can go if you want to."

They stood watching Zeely but kept their distance from her. Razorbacks and great brute hogs, some weighing as much as four hundred pounds, milled around her like so many little children.

"She doesn't seem to mind them at all," Geeder said.

The hogs made angry snorts at Geeder and Toeboy, however, sensing that the two didn't belong there.

All at once, there was a flurry of movement among the animals. Zeely moved about in her graceful, aloof way. She collected all the empty pails as though she meant to leave.

"Zeely!" Geeder shouted. "Aren't you going to move the animals today?" Her voice surprised her. It was quite loud in the quiet field.

Geeder never found out what Zeely answered. Zeely had turned toward her when an unearthly squeal came from Uncle Ross' barn. Zeely walked over to the broken fence and weighted it down with heavy rocks so that the smaller pigs couldn't root under it. Then she made her way from the field, swinging the gate closed behind her. She headed down Leadback Road, passed Uncle Ross' house and did not look to the left or to the right. Geeder watched her go out of sight, wondering about her, hoping she would turn around. Zeely didn't do anything more than walk away down the road.

When Toeboy and Geeder reached the barn, they found Uncle Ross filling in a hole he had dug.

"What's that hole for?" Toeboy asked.

"Entrails of the sow," Uncle Ross said. Seeing Geeder's questioning face, he motioned her and

Toeboy toward the barn door. "You'll find her in there," he said.

Inside the barn they found the sow. "Why, they've butchered her!" Geeder said. The sow was already skinned and hanging high overhead on an oak crossbeam. The carcass was bloody red. Geeder had to turn her face away.

"I hope I don't have to eat any of that," Toeboy said. He gulped hard, for the sight of the raw meat made him sick.

"Oh, I couldn't eat it, I just couldn't!" Geeder said.

"You two get away, now," Uncle Ross said, coming up behind them. "Go to the shed where there's something for you to do."

"But I want to see Mr. Tayber move his hogs," Geeder said.

"Well, he won't be moving them today," said Uncle Ross. "Too much time lost because of the sow. He'll have to move them tomorrow. You go on to the shed. There's plenty for you to do there."

The day before, Uncle Ross had told them what he wanted them to do in the shed. They were to stack magazines and catalogs in neat bundles and tie them so they could be carted away. Geeder and Toeboy were more than glad to leave the barn. They rushed out into the sunlight, leaving the sad carcass of the sow and the memory of it behind.

Geeder had an odd feeling whenever she entered the shed. It was cool and shadowy, always. Both she and Toeboy were barefoot and the earthen floor of the shed felt clean and fresh. The whole place made whispering seem quite natural. The roof was louvered boards, over which a large tarpaulin was fastened in bad weather. Today, the tarpaulin was folded away and long stripes of sunlight slanted to the floor. The sun got tangled in dust and cobwebs and glowed in dark corners. All was still. What little noise Geeder and Toeboy made was muffled, fading quickly. They took a good look around before settling down to work.

They sat close together. Toeboy stacked the catalogs, and Geeder had the magazines.

"I love going through old pictures," Geeder said. "It's the best fun of anything."

"It's not fair," Toeboy said. "You could let me have some of the magazines."

"Well, you can't have any," Geeder said. "Just do what you're supposed to and be quiet about it."

Toeboy was mad enough at Geeder to hit her. But he knew she would start a fight if he did and she would probably win, too. He contented himself with the catalogs. He had two bundles of fifty stacked and tied before Geeder had stacked any magazines.

"You're not supposed to read them," he told her. "That's not fair at all."

"I'm just looking at the pictures before I stack them," she said.

"You'd better not let Uncle Ross catch you."

"You worry so much about nothing!" Geeder said.

"I believe I'll just go tell Uncle Ross," Toeboy said. He got up, heading for the door. Geeder smiled after him and continued turning the glossy pages of a magazine.

Toeboy stood at the corner of the shed. He waited for Geeder to come after him but she didn't. He stood, fidgeting and trying hard to be quiet. Finally, he came back inside. He knew instantly that something was wrong.

Geeder bent low over a magazine. On her lap were two more magazines that slowly slid to the floor. She pressed her hand against the page, as if to hold on to what she saw there. Then, she sat very still and her breath came in a long, low sigh.

"Geeder?" Toeboy whispered. "I'm not going to tell. I was only teasing you."

She didn't hear him. He crept up beside her and tried taking the magazine from her, but she wouldn't let it go. He looked over her shoulder. What he saw caused him to leap away, as though he had seen a ghost.

"I knew it all the time! I knew it!" Geeder said to him.

Geeder had found something extraordinary, a photograph of an African woman of royal birth. She was a Mututsi. She belonged to the Batutsi tribe. The magazine Geeder held said that the Batutsis were so tall they were almost giants. They were known all over the world as Watutsis, the word for them in the Swahili language. Except for the tribal gown the girl wore and the royal headband wound tightly around her head, she could have been Zeely Tayber standing tall and serene in Uncle Ross' west field.

Toeboy carefully read what was written under the photograph of the African girl. "Maybe Zeely Tayber is a queen," he said at last.

Geeder stared at Toeboy. It took her a few seconds to compose herself enough to say, "Well, of course, Toeboy—what do you think? I never doubted for a minute that Miss Zeely Tayber was anything else!"

She was quiet a long while then, staring at the photograph. It was as if her mind had left her. She simply sat with her mouth open, holding the picture; not one whisper passed her lips.

Uncle Ross happened by the shed. He didn't see Geeder and Toeboy at first, they sat so still in the shadows. But soon, his eyes grew accustomed to the darkness of the shed as he peeked in and he smiled and entered. Geeder aroused herself, getting up to meet Uncle Ross. She handed him the magazine without a word. Uncle Ross carried it to the doorway; there, in the light, he stood gazing at the photograph. His face grew puzzled. Geeder was to remember all day and all night what he said at that moment.

"The same nose," he muttered, "those slanted eyes . . . black, too, black as night." He looked from the photograph to Geeder, then to Toeboy and back to Geeder again. "So you believe Zeely

Tayber to be some kind of royalty," he said, finally.

"There isn't any doubt that Zeely's a queen," Geeder said. Her voice was calm. "The picture is proof."

"You may have discovered the people Zeely is descended from," Uncle Ross said, "but I can't see that that's going to make her a queen." He was about to say more when he noticed Geeder's stubborn expression. He knew then that anything he might say would make no difference. He left the shed without saying anything else. And when he had gone, Geeder danced around with the photograph clutched in her arms. Toeboy hopped on one foot the length of the shed.

"Oh, it's just grand," Geeder said. "Everything was left to me and I took care of it all by myself!"

8

That afternoon, Geeder stayed in her room gazing at the photograph of the Watutsi woman. Toeboy disappeared right after lunch and Uncle Ross had business in the village. Geeder studied the picture from a distance, from up close and from every angle. She sat stiffly in one of the cherry-wood chairs in her room, running her hands slowly over its arms. Her heart beat so fast she felt she would faint.

Soon, she tried standing as straight and tall as the woman in the photograph stood. But she didn't feel right standing that way.

"My neck isn't long enough," she said. "My arms are too short."

Geeder stretched out on her bed and looked out through the luster and glitter of her beads. She saw herself, tall and very thin, walking with Zeely

Tayber. They were sisters. They looked so much
alike that people sometimes called her Zeely.
Zeely Tayber was queen but she liked having
Geeder always at her side. Anytime people
wanted to talk with Zeely, they first had to speak
with Geeder. She would listen and then she would
give Zeely a sign and Zeely would understand.
Zeely could not talk to anyone but Geeder, that
was the law of the land. One night Zeely was very
sick. Everyone thought she surely would die. It
was Geeder who got her well again in just one
week. And then, Zeely was so happy, she made
Geeder queen.

"Queen," Geeder said, out loud. She turned on
her side so she could see the photograph of the
Watutsi woman.

"It's a pretty picture," she said. "It's about the
nicest picture I've ever seen."

By suppertime, Toeboy had returned to the
farm. Uncle Ross had come home, too, and he prepared a wonderful dinner for them. There was
baked chicken allowed to cool, sweet potatoes,
beans from the pantry and a salad of fresh vegeta-
bles from the garden. By suppertime, also, Geeder
had made up her mind about something. She had
never gone to any of the bonfires the children
were fond of having. They loved nothing better
than dried weeds and corncobs smoking high and
burning bright. They danced and sang around the
flames until they were too tired even to sleep.

There was to be a bonfire tonight. This time,
she would go. She ate quickly and spoke little,

saying just enough to let Uncle Ross know that the sweet potatoes were fine. She just couldn't get enough sweet potatoes, she told him.

"Can Geeder and I go to Bennie Green's house this evening?" Toeboy asked right after they had finished eating. Beyond Bennie's back yard was an empty lot where the bonfire would be. Nearly all the children of the farms and the town were going to be there.

"I'll let you go," Uncle Ross said, "but you must be home by eleven o'clock."

"Oh, Uncle Ross!" Toeboy pleaded. "The sky doesn't even turn dark until after nine—that's no time at all!"

"No good bonfire can blaze good if the sky isn't black," Geeder said.

Uncle Ross thought a minute. "Twelve o'clock, then," he said, "but no later. And be careful of the flames. Don't get smoke in your eyes!"

He knew they would come home with their clothing singed; their skin and hair would smell of smoke for days to come. But Archibald Green, Bennie's father, would keep a sharp eye out so that none of the children would harm themselves.

Nine fifteen, and the sky was deepest black with a moon full and red above the fields.

"Look what's walking along with us," Toeboy said. The moon was so clear that Geeder and Toeboy cast shadows as they hurried along Leadback Road.

"I can hear the kids at the bonfire," Geeder said, "and we still have a long way to go."

They could see the bonfire. It lit up all the houses and trees in that part of town where Bennie Green lived. Soon, they left Leadback Road to shortcut through back yards, following fence lines directly to the bonfire.

The children ranged around the fire. They were bright Indians; some had feathers in their hair. Here, a face was weirdly lighted, and there, a whole figure emerged only to become lost in shadow as though it had never been. As Geeder and Toeboy climbed the last fence, a green and gold stream of sparks rose high above the flames.

"Isn't that pretty!" Geeder whispered. "Why, everything is just beautiful for Zeely and me!"

Bennie Green came over to greet Geeder and Toeboy and so did some of the other children.

Geeder wore ten strands of glass beads of every color, shape and size. The flames reflected in the glass, causing her neck to seem encircled by stars. The girls greatly admired the necklaces, as they did Geeder. They had seen her before, but she hadn't often played with them; that was why they were somewhat shy with her. She was different, that was all. She lived away in a city and they believed she must know a great many things. This night, Geeder was nice to them.

"You can take turns wearing my necklaces," she said.

This pleased the girls, and Geeder, too.

When the bonfire died down to a few feet above the coals, Bennie Green passed out two hotdogs, two buns and a stick to each person. There was lemonade to drink and soon all of them were busy eating. The girls bunched together right next to the boys. Geeder got talking about Zeely Tayber. Before she knew it, she was telling a story. Even the boys listened to her.

She was aware of the silence around her and saw the darkness within the trees, where the bonfire could not penetrate.

"Zeely Tayber is a queen," she said, "and this picture I found is her grandmother as a girl."

Toeboy acted as though he wanted to say something. Geeder gave him a hard look so he wouldn't utter a word. From her pocket, she brought out the photograph of the Watutsi woman. It was passed from hand to hand, with the girls and boys leaning close to the fire to see it.

"I bet Miss Zeely looks exactly like her mother," Geeder said. "And her mother looked just like *her* mother, and on and on, clear to Africa, where it all began."

Geeder was interrupted by a boy called Warner. He was tall and thin, taller than the other boys. He stood up, hopping back and forth on one foot. "I know about Watutsis," he said. "They come from a place once called Ruanda-Urundi. It has a new name now because it's a new nation. I know all about them and they are bad people. They keep people as slaves!"

The boys and girls sat silently, looking from Warner to Geeder. Geeder said that she didn't believe him, that he must have made the whole thing up. But Warner wasn't to be taken lightly. He told a sad tale of the troubles of the Watutsis. He said that their former slaves had risen to fight them, that soon there might not be any Watutsis.

"Well," said Geeder, "you shouldn't speak mean of them if they're being hurt. Anyway, I don't see what that has to do with Zeely. She's still the same. She's still a queen!"

"You're a silly girl," Warner said, seriously,

"and I'm going home." He whistled for his dog and the two of them ran down Leadback Road. The boy whistled and the dog yapped all the way across town.

When Warner had gone, Geeder forgot him and all he said. She didn't have to say that Zeely was a queen again because by now everyone knew how important Zeely really was.

"Tomorrow," she said, "Zeely's going to move all the prize razorbacks down to Red Barn and I wouldn't miss seeing her do that for the world!"

A short while after Geeder ended her story, leaves and corncobs were once more heaped on the bonfire. The flames shot high into the air. The boys and girls started leaping and dancing, making enough noise to be heard for miles.

Toeboy joined in the fun. Right away, he started the game of daring the flames with his clothing.

Geeder was left alone. "How can they play like that when so much is to happen in the morning?" she said to herself. "Toeboy's the worst one of all. He could have sat with me to keep me company."

She got up and quietly collected her necklaces from the girls. Then she left the bonfire without saying good-bye to anyone.

When Toeboy noticed that Geeder had gone, he at once headed for home. Nearly at the farm, he overtook her.

"Guess what I saw?" Geeder said. She had forgotten she was angry with him for leaving her alone.

"What?" asked Toeboy.

"I saw a circle around the moon," Geeder said. "See?" She pointed up through the trees where the moon was going down. It looked like a cold, yellow eye.

"There's a circle, all right," Toeboy said. "I bet there'll be mist in the morning."

"Of course there will be," Geeder said, "and it will fit just fine with what's to happen."

"What's to happen?" Toeboy wanted to know.

"Why, Zeely!" Geeder said. "Zeely parading all those animals into town—what in the world did you think I meant!"

Geeder and Toeboy lay under a dark sky that night. The moon went away and the stars seemed hard and far off. Toeboy slept fitfully and Geeder stared into the night. Under the covers with her lay Uncle Ross' flashlight. She did not touch it; she hardly realized it was beside her. Any thought of the night traveller had drifted far back in her mind. She slipped into a sound sleep.

Geeder did not dream or speak out in the night, nor did she witness the passing of the night traveller down Leadback Road. But Toeboy did. Perhaps it was the excitement of the bonfire that caused him to turn and toss in his sleep. He awoke several times, turned, saw that Geeder was asleep and went back to sleep himself. Maybe it was the fact that the night traveller did not only walk down Leadback Road this night. Before it passed the hedge in front of the house, it paused for as much as thirty seconds. It seemed to listen; perhaps it waited. Whatever its reason for stopping there in the road, it did so when Toeboy had awakened from a dream of bright fires.

He couldn't have said why he crawled all the way out of the lilac bush and sat there with his toes touching the wet grass. It wasn't just to see if Geeder was still asleep. Maybe he had heard some sound or maybe he thought he was still at the bonfire, for the bright, clear faces of his friends, the smell of smoke and the shape of the flames were with him still. Toeboy saw the thing at the hedge right away. It stood where the hedge parted, at the foot of the path leading to the house. It had no arms or legs. He knew at once what he saw, and he wasn't afraid.

"Good evening, Miss Zeely," he said, softly. "How do you do?"

Zeely Tayber turned slightly toward the place where Geeder slept. She made a movement as though to silence Toeboy. Then, she glided on down Leadback Road and the darkness of the night was all there was.

10

Before daybreak, a fog rose from the hollows and fanned out through the catalpa trees. It lay like smoke over swimming holes. When Geeder and Toeboy awoke at six thirty, it covered all the land. The whole town and countryside was trapped in a thick fog, too warm and wet to be anything other than strange. They found their bedding soaked. Even their clothing, which they had slept in in order to save time in the morning, was uncomfortably damp.

Toeboy was about to tell Geeder that he had seen Zeely Tayber come down the road in the night when she whispered excitedly, "Toeboy, it's begun!"

And so it had begun. Nat Tayber had started his prize animals down Leadback Road. Toeboy for-

got to tell how Zeely looked in the darkness and
Geeder forgot to feed Uncle Ross' chickens. They
ran to the elm tree near the road and climbed to
the top. There, they could see perfectly and not be
seen. They saw Uncle Ross hurry out of the house,
look around for them and then wait by the road.
From their vantage point they could see above the
mist. Suddenly, the sun broke through and the top
of the mist was spread with gold.

It was seven o'clock by the time Nat Tayber
and his hogs reached the elm tree. Uncle Ross
stood nearby, hoping, perhaps, that Nat would
need him to help move the animals. Nat didn't, of
course. He had hired strong, husky lads from the
village.

"The mood he's in," Geeder whispered, "he
won't ask Uncle Ross for anything."

"He's got mud all over him," Toeboy said.

"I bet he fell chasing one of the hogs. Oh, does
he look mean!" Geeder said.

Nat Tayber was covered with mud from the
chest down. In one hand, he carried a long prodding pole. All the boys he had hired were
equipped with the same sort of poles.

"I don't see Zeely," said Geeder. "She ought to
be right in front." All she could see through the
mist was the trail of animals and Nat Tayber and
his boys. Suddenly, Geeder found Zeely far back
at the end of the line of animals.

"Why, what's she doing way back there?"
Geeder whispered. Zeely moved slowly in and out

of the mist, never once hurrying and never speaking. She wore a long, white smock that reached to her feet.

Toeboy recognized the smock Zeely wore. It was what had made her appear to have no arms or feet or head the night before. The smock was streaked with mud.

"She's got herself all dirty," he said. "She's about as muddy as old Nat."

"Hush, Toeboy!" Geeder whispered. "I don't care if she is dirty. Just look at her! Oh, she's pretty, with all that mist around her!"

Zeely Tayber carried a pail of feed instead of a prodding pole. Whenever one of the huge razorbacks stopped for too long, she held the pail under its snout. As it ate, she walked forward again until the animal was moving. It was a slow process but it worked well. Still, the hogs took their time.

"I bet Nat thinks he's going to get those hogs through town before it's full of trucks and cars," Geeder said to Toeboy.

"He won't make it," Toeboy said, "not the rate he's going."

"It'll serve him right for not letting Zeely lead," Geeder said. "Can't you just see the street packed with folks and those animals and Nat and all those boys trying to get through?"

On Leadback Road, some of Nat Tayber's hogs got going in the wrong direction; others lay down by Uncle Ross' hedge to rest. The boys he had hired rushed to the hedge, hitting the tired animals with their poles. When the first blow was struck, Geeder held her breath. Finally, she had to turn her face away.

"That's no way to treat hogs," Uncle Ross hollered. "Those are prize animals—that's no way!"

Nat Tayber ignored him. "Hit them! Hit them!" he yelled to the boys. "That will make them move!"

The animals rose, squealing frantically, and lumbered away down the road toward the village. The rest of the hogs followed as fast as their great bulk would let them. Nat and the boys ran after the hogs.

Through it all, Geeder had watched silently. She felt sick when the animals were hit so hard and sorry when they were forced to run down Leadback Road. And now, she was left with a sour taste on her tongue.

"Goodness knows, animals shouldn't be hurt by anyone," she whispered to herself.

She felt like not going into town, fearing to see the animals beaten again. Then, Zeely passed by the tree. She did not seem to be a part of what had happened, nor to be aware of the press of smelling, dirty animals around her. Geeder whistled so Zeely would look up and see her.

Once she sees me, Geeder thought, I know she'll want me to help.

Zeely Tayber paused. But then she went on, as silent and serene as ever. Toeboy and Geeder watched her disappear into the mist.

Geeder guessed Zeely hadn't heard her. "Maybe when she gets into town and sees me there . . ."

she whispered, not quite able to finish the wish, even to herself. She and Toeboy climbed down the tree and raced for the catalpa trees. There was a shorter route through the forest to town.

They were more than halfway along, running fast, when Toeboy thought about seeing Zeely Tayber.

"I saw Miss Zeely last night," he began. "And Geeder, it was very late, I know it was because I was so sleepy. She looked just as funny, like she didn't have any arms or anything. That was because the night was so dark."

Geeder stopped dead in her tracks. She was panting hard and her eyes were too wide, as though she hadn't enough light to see. "What did you say?" she whispered.

"I just said that Miss Zeely came down the road last night," Toeboy said, catching his breath.

Geeder stared at him and slowly nodded her head. "The other part," she said softly, "how did you say she looked?"

"She looked funny, that's all," Toeboy said. He fidgeted uncomfortably under Geeder's gaze. "See, she had on that long dress she was wearing today and it made her seem to glide. I couldn't see her face. And that bucket she carried floated with her." He laughed. "That was because I couldn't see her arms."

"Bucket?" Geeder said. Her voice made hardly a sound.

"The feed pail," Toeboy said. "I guess she was

coming from feeding the hogs. Geeder, what's the matter?"

Geeder sat down, hard, on the ground. "Oh, Toeboy!" she said. She covered her face with her hands and rocked back and forth. "Oh, my goodness, Toeboy! That wasn't Zeely Tayber you saw. That was the night traveller!"

As soon as she said the words, Geeder had a clear vision of the night traveller, the time she had seen it. It had had no arms or legs, no head. It was a thing that moved right on the air and Toeboy had seen it. A shiver ran up her spine.

"Toeboy!" she said. "You saw a night traveller and no one is ever supposed to see one!"

Geeder looked so terrified that all of a sudden Toeboy was aware of the wet, misty trees surrounding them. The catalpas were so dense they could have been a solid wall. Anything could hide within them, just there, where it was as dark as night. He felt his back grow cold.

"I thought it was just Zeely Tayber," he said.

"No," Geeder said.

"It stopped right by the path to the house," Toeboy said.

"Toeboy, did it do anything?" Geeder asked.

Toeboy nodded, watching the trees. He crouched next to Geeder and his voice began to tremble as he spoke. "I thought it was going to say something," he said. "I was sitting right out in front of the lilac bush and it was looking at me. And you know what it did, Geeder?"

"What?" she said. She put one hand on his shoulder, pulling him closer.

"It moved real funny," he said, "and I got the feeling it didn't want me to say anything. I guess it didn't like noise."

"Oh, Toeboy!" Geeder said. "Can you just think what it would have done if you had made a sound!"

Toeboy tried to swallow but he couldn't. He remembered he had said good evening to what he thought was Miss Zeely Tayber. "What do you think it would have done?" he asked.

"Why, it would come back some night," Geeder said. "It would wait until you were asleep!"

An awful fear welled inside Toeboy. The night traveller was sure to get him because he had talked to it. He wanted to get away from the old trees around him and Geeder. He wanted to be as close to Uncle Ross as he could get.

All at once, Geeder jumped to her feet and started to run. Toeboy fell flat on the ground and covered his head with his arms. His eyes were closed tight and Geeder, seeing him, had to laugh.

"Silly!" she called. "Nothing's going to get you in broad daylight. It's the hog drive—did you forget?"

Toeboy lifted his head.

"There's Zeely to see," Geeder said. "And don't you worry about the night traveller. You just stay close to me."

11

"Just look at all the people!" Geeder had not thought so many folks could fit on the main street. The mood was right for a parade. The children were all there, the ones who had been at the bonfire the night before and still others who had heard the story of Zeely.

"Let's get closer!" Geeder grabbed Toeboy by the arm and pushed her way through the children at the curbs until she was right in front. Now she could see all the folks talking in small groups at the corner. They would glance curiously at the children and then quickly away.

"They don't want us to know why they're here," she said, "but I know why. They've come to see Zeely just like we have!"

Before Nat Tayber reached the center of the village, the air held the smell of hogs. The scent caught in the mist not yet evaporated by the sun. Wild, piercing squeals cut through the musky odor as Nat and his boys used their poles. Geeder shivered and crossed her fingers so the animals would not get hurt badly. People poured forth from stores and shops, taking up positions on both sides of the street. There were women in bonnets against the mist, with loaded shopping bags and baskets. There were farm people in their coveralls and wide-brim hats. There were all kinds of people there—townspeople, country folk and hordes of near-hysterical boys and girls, unable to speak for fear they might spoil what was to come.

"Geeder, I'm going," Toeboy said. "I want to go back to Uncle Ross."

"Toeboy, what's wrong with you?" Geeder said. She couldn't believe she had heard him right.

"I don't *like* it here," he said, "and I don't want to see those animals hurt." He was thinking about the night traveller and wondering what it would do when it caught up with him.

"Oh, don't be dumb, Toeboy! They won't get hurt," Geeder said. "Zeely won't let them get hurt. You stay right where you are."

"How will she keep them from getting hurt?" Toeboy asked.

"She won't let them, that's all," Geeder said. "Don't you worry."

"Let me go," Toeboy pleaded. "I don't want to see the hogs run any more."

Geeder ignored him, holding on to him tightly as the hogs came on in a mass.

"There's the mist over everything," she whispered to herself. "It makes the street all wet and shining. Look how the sun comes through in patches. There's not a thing to say about it, it's a special day to the stars. Zeely Tayber is the brightest star of all!"

The hogs looked as if they were half crazed from fear. Many of them frothed at the mouth and staggered blindly in circles. Nat Tayber and his boys managed to get in front of them to slow the lead animals down. It was a wonder the boys and Nat didn't get bitten, for the hogs snapped at and fought anything that got in their path.

All the time, Toeboy struggled to free himself, but Geeder grimly held him. The odor and sight of the frightened, exhausted animals sickened her.

"They'll be all right," she said softly to Toeboy. "You'll see, nobody will hurt them."

Through the street passed Zeely Tayber, her long smock brilliant in the mist. She moved straight and tall. Often, a fresh gust of breeze billowed the smock, causing her to appear to rise above the animals. She was taller than any of the men along the curbs and taller than the young trees lining the street. Through all the terrific noise and brutal movement, she made no sudden motion, nor did her face change from its serenity.

"Oh, she's just wonderful!" Geeder whispered. "She's just the most beautiful lady!"

And so Zeely was. She was beautiful and tall and unlike anyone else in the whole town.

Suddenly an enormous sow fell. She frothed at

the mouth and grunted, as though something hurt
her. Other hogs trampled her and still she was unable to move.

"That's awful!" Geeder said. "Oh, somebody do
something!"

Toeboy jerked free from Geeder and instantly
disappeared back in the crowd.

"Well, you just go home then," Geeder muttered.

Someone was shouting, "A sow's fallen! A sow's
fallen!" The injured sow still lay grunting in the
street. Other folks began shouting the same thing,
and in a while, Nat Tayber raced back through
the animals.

Something happened to Geeder when she saw
Nat heading for the sow. Her face grew burning
hot and her arms felt cold. She was in the street
before she knew it. She was going away from Nat
toward Zeely, who was still at the rear of the line
of animals.

Geeder could hear people shouting at her to get
out of the way before she was trampled. Once,
somebody reached for her. She felt the sharp prick
of fingernails as she pulled away. All of them, the
people shouting and the one person who had tried
to hold her back, seemed far away. She didn't
think about anything except hurrying.

She was running. She got in the way of a hog.
Some animals snapped at her, knocking into her;
she was crying a little, from somewhere in her
throat. There was pain in her left foot where a big
boar had stepped on her. The stench of the ani-

mals made her legs weak. She almost fell, but then
Zeely was just ahead. Geeder had to step between
two sows to get to her. She placed her hand as
lightly as she could on the back of one animal in
order to get around it. The heat of the hog shot up
her arm and she gasped in terror.

The crowd roared in Geeder's mind. She
couldn't think what they were saying because the
sound ebbed and rose, like many voices over the
radio when there is too much static.

Miss Zeely was standing still. Miss Zeely was
staring at her.

Zeely Tayber moved to shield Geeder from the
hogs. She didn't touch Geeder, but leaned over
her. Geeder started talking before Zeely had a
chance to warn her out of the way of the hogs.

"It's a sow," Geeder said. She rested one hand
on her knee, trying to catch her breath. "It's all
sick in the street, just lying down. Nat . . . your
father. He's got his pole!"

Geeder straightened up too quickly. There was
a stitch in her side that took her breath away. She
had to bend down and come up slowly before the
pain eased. Then, Zeely had Geeder by the arm.

Zeely was walking fast. She leaned forward like
a young tree bent in a storm. She walked as
though she had made a path through the animals
and not one animal touched her, nor Geeder, either. Not more than a half minute had passed
since the time Geeder had begun to run and Zeely
had started back with her through the hogs. In no
time, they saw Nat Tayber prodding the stricken

sow hard with his pole. Zeely stopped a few feet from Nat. She let go of Geeder, gently, one finger at a time. Geeder watched Zeely's eyes empty of strain and fill with something that glinted and flared.

The sow lay grunting under Nat's prodding. She could not move. Then, his face frozen in an awful grimace, Nat Tayber raised the prodding pole high above his head. Before he could bring it down on the sow, Zeely was there beside him.

Zeely grabbed Nat's wrist. The pole stood poised and trembling in the air and mist. Zeely looked long and hard at Nat. Her lips moved as she spoke softly to him. Nat twisted the pole. It jerked toward Zeely's head and then, slowly, came down to rest at Nat's side. In a second, Nat had turned on his heel. He was gone to lead the animals, not once glancing at the crowd.

The crowd hushed. At once, the stench of the hogs was overpowering. Geeder felt sick and dizzy. She dug her nails in her palms and breathed in short, quick gasps.

Zeely Tayber bent down beside the stricken sow. As if on a string, the people lining the street bent down at the same moment. Up and down the sidewalks, people were squatting or kneeling. They could have been praying there, they were so quiet, watching Zeely.

Geeder knelt down beside Zeely. She took Zeely's feed pail on her lap and held it at an angle so Zeely could reach into it. Geeder forgot the hog

smell and all the people watching, so close was she
to Zeely Tayber.

Zeely took a bit of feed from the pail and held it
in her hand out to the sow. The sow feebly lifted
her head and ate from Zeely's hand.

A soft murmur passed along the street. It
reached Geeder and went through her, in and out
of her, draining her of her strength. She felt weak.

Now, the sow struggled to get up. Soon, it was
able to walk. Zeely took the feed pail from Geeder
without a word. She did so carefully, graciously,
and walked away.

"It's all right," Geeder murmured, as if Zeely
had thanked her. "I thought you might need me to
help."

The sow followed along at Zeely's heels like a
pet of some kind. Zeely no longer needed to hold
out her hand with the feed. She simply lowered
the pail, allowing the sow to eat. All the way to
Red Barn, the sow tagged along behind Zeely. She
waited while Zeely got other hogs up and moving,
for many more had fallen. She stumbled close behind when Zeely moved quickly along.

The people watching couldn't believe what they
saw happen in front of their eyes. Geeder stood
among them, listening to what was said and
watching Zeely and the hogs move out of sight.

"That Tayber girl has bewitched the sow," some
people said.

"It is because she is animal, like those hogs."
People snickered and laughed.

Many voices caught and whirled in Geeder's

mind. She grew angry and pushed her way out of the crowd.

Geeder trotted, limping, to Uncle Ross' farm. She was still weak, bruised and slightly sick to her stomach. But the air had cleared. The mist, thick as smoke, had risen and gone. By the time she passed through the catalpa trees, the smell and danger of hogs had left her. Zeely Tayber was with her still, deep in her thoughts.

"I helped her," Geeder whispered. "I knew she'd want me to."

12

Geeder and Toeboy burst into the house to tell Uncle Ross what they had heard in town. It was Tuesday, three days after Nat Tayber's hog run down Leadback Road.

"All the folks say Nat didn't get a good price for his animals," Geeder said.

"Because they were beaten and run so hard to market," Toeboy added.

"Is that so?" Uncle Ross said. "Well, Nat should have known better than to treat prize hogs the way he did."

"Will you still get your share?" asked Geeder.

"Maybe I won't take my share," Uncle Ross said. "I never use that west field for anything."

Nat Tayber was a proud man. He told everyone he had made a good profit from the sale of his hogs, and perhaps he had. Later that day, he came by the farm and left the money with Geeder when Uncle Ross was in town.

Now, only Nat came down the road to the west field to care for what animals remained. Geeder found no great joy in watching him each morning. She was pressed to find things to do. She decided to tell Nat about the photograph she had discovered and what she had come to believe about Zeely.

Geeder leaned on the west-field fence, watching Nat feed baby pigs and brute hogs. "What if he laughs?" she wondered. "Worse, still, what if he turns on me—he can get mean with people." It was no use. She could not work up the courage to talk to Nat about Zeely.

She heard a car come down Leadback Road and turned from the field in time to see a green coupe stop in front of the farmhouse. Uncle Ross went out to the car. In a little while, the car drove off the way it had come. Geeder guessed that it was just some gentleman to see Uncle Ross. She didn't even mention the car to Toeboy when he returned from playing at Bennie Green's and came into her room.

"We're building a tree house at Bennie Green's," he said.

Geeder made no comment about it.

"I can take you to see it after we eat," he said, but still Geeder showed no interest.

"Geeder, what's wrong with you?"

"Toeboy, I'm thinking," she told him, "and I'll thank you not to bother me."

He left her alone, somewhat hurt by the change in her. He thought of writing a letter to his father about Geeder. She didn't seem like Geeder at all. She was more like Elizabeth Perry, who she was, really. He hadn't thought of her as Elizabeth all summer. Since Saturday, the day Nat Tayber sold his hogs, Toeboy had had to find others to play with from morning until night. All that Tuesday Geeder just stayed in her room. She never suggested that they sleep outside any more. He was glad of that. He wouldn't sleep out of doors again and chance seeing the night traveller a second time for anything in the world. Something told him the night traveller would never come in the house to get him; but, of course, he couldn't be sure. Still, it was funny that Geeder didn't want to sleep out.

No, since Saturday, she hadn't been like Geeder at all. In fact, she was just like any other girl.

He was thinking again about the night traveller and how he could protect himself from it when he found Uncle Ross in the dining room. Uncle Ross was seated, waxing the dining-room table with a white cloth. His arm moved in long, circular sweeps. He had the dining-room light on. The light hung from a single chain from the ceiling, just above Uncle Ross' head. Its shade was shaped like a bell and was made of pretty colored glass which reflected in nice patterns on Uncle Ross' arm. Toeboy sat down at the table to watch, careful not to touch the fresh wax.

Uncle Ross didn't say hello and neither did

Toeboy. Toeboy never had to say anything to Uncle Ross if he didn't want to. That was why he liked him so much. He could sit beside Uncle Ross forever and a Sunday and Uncle Ross would never make him talk. Sometimes, Uncle Ross would talk out loud and often he would tell about things Toeboy had never heard of.

"Old oak tables," Uncle Ross said quietly. "Round, with maybe a hundred years of people using them." His hand swept in and out of the light. "They are like old people," he said. "They need a care and a handling that is gentle, the way my mother used to stir a little love into her cooking." Uncle Ross chuckled and fell silent again. The table gleamed with polish but still his arm swept around and around.

"You don't think a night traveller would ever come inside a body's house, do you, Uncle Ross?" Toeboy asked. "I mean, when he was sleeping, when all the doors were locked?"

"The doors of this house are never locked," Uncle Ross said, "and what are you talking about in the first place?"

"I'm talking about night travellers," Toeboy said.

"You first must tell me what night travellers are," Uncle Ross said.

Toeboy was silent, surprised that Uncle Ross didn't know. Maybe he had forgotten. "Geeder says that dark roads are walked by night travellers late at night."

"Geeder says, does she?" Uncle Ross said.

"Well, then, it must be so. Let me think about it for just a minute."

Toeboy absently pressed his fingers on the smooth table. Seeing his fingerprints there in the wax, he jerked his hand away.

"It's all right," Uncle Ross said. "That's what you're supposed to do."

"But it marks it all up," Toeboy said.

"What do you think folks did a long time ago," Uncle Ross said, "when there was maybe a whole family of eight or ten sitting around this table? They would laugh and talk, joke and tell tales." Uncle Ross smiled to himself. "They'd smooth their palms over a table like this every day, three times a day. Maybe they'd sit at the table all day long in the winter when there wasn't any other heat but what came from the cook-stove in the kitchen. After some years had caught the wind, that table would shine and it would shine from the oil out of their hands."

"Uncle Ross, is that a true story?" Toeboy asked.

"It is," Uncle Ross said.

They were silent. Uncle Ross switched hands. Toeboy crossed his arms on the table and rested his chin on them. Uncle Ross' hand swept close to Toeboy's face in a steady rhythm.

"Night travellers, you say?" Uncle Ross said. "Night travellin'."

He began to hum under his breath. It was a throaty sound. Soon, he began to sing in a voice that had all but forgotten such work.

> *"Night travellin', Night travellin'*
> *I step my feet down strong,*
> *I'm Night travellin'"*

As he began to recall the words, his voice grew stronger and the deep tones of the song caught the rhythm of his hand upon the table.

"That's a tune!" Toeboy said. "That's about night travellers!"

"Slaves used to sing that," Uncle Ross said. "That was how they told one another in the fields that they planned to get away from slavery."

"Are there other songs like that?" Toeboy wanted to know.

Uncle Ross nodded. "There's the song about the drinking gourd," he said. "Slaves called the Big Dipper the drinking gourd so folks wouldn't know what they were talking about. The Big Dipper stars lay in the north sky and the slaves would follow them out of the south to Canada."

"How does it go?" Toeboy asked.

"Well," Uncle Ross said, clearing his throat, "it tells about this man with a wooden leg. The slaves never saw him but they'd follow the mark of his wooden leg through forest trails and along river-banks—

> *"There's a river runs between two trees*
> *There's another river on the other side*
> *Left foot, peg foot, travel along,*
> *Follow the drinking gourd.*

"And there's still another one," Uncle Ross said. "*I'm just a poor, wayfarin' stranger,*" he sang, "*travellin' through this land of woe.* There's the 'Long John' song. Prison men used to sing that one. It told about Long John, how he was going to run.

> "*I'm Long John, I'm long gone*
> *Like a turkey through the corn*
> *With my long clothes on*
> *I'm Long John, I'm long gone, I'm*
>   *gone gone.*"

"Then a night traveller is a slave or a prison man?" Toeboy asked. He reached out, placing his hand over Uncle Ross'. Their hands moved together through the many lights reflected on the table, Toeboy's smooth and small and Uncle Ross' creased with summer and fall and many new years.

"I believe," Uncle Ross began, "a night traveller must be somebody who wants to walk tall. And to walk tall, you most certainly must have to run free. Yes," he said, "it is the free spirit in any of us breaking loose."

"I saw a night traveller," Toeboy said, softly. "It was late at night, after the big bonfire at Bennie Green's. It came down the road just like a ghost. I thought it was Miss Zeely Tayber."

Uncle Ross smiled. "Zeely Tayber comes down the road at night to check on those hogs. You most likely saw her."

"Geeder took your flashlight," Toeboy said. "She doesn't know I know but I saw it in her room. I bet she's seen the night traveller, too, and means to shine the flashlight on it. And when she does, I bet it won't be Zeely Tayber, no sir!"

"So," Uncle Ross said, "let thy little light shine on the lonesome traveller and the night—" He chuckled and let the thought go.

He and Toeboy leaned together on one side of the big oak table. The light fell fully on them, leaving the rest of the room in growing shadow. They were there, full of the warmth of tales and talk, when two hands floated out of the darkness. The fingertips came to rest on the gleaming table. They could have been hewn from stone.

Uncle Ross' hand jerked to a halt. Toeboy gasped, feeling Uncle Ross' arm tense as strong and hard as a plank of wood. Their eyes were glued to the hands without arms across the table. Toeboy tried to cry out but his voice was gone. It was the traveller come to get him, for what but the traveller could have come so quickly out of the dark?

"And the night?" a small voice said, "and the night?" repeating the last words Uncle Ross had spoken.

The lone hands had arms. Geeder sat down at the table.

Uncle Ross sighed. "And the night," he said, "as dark as the color of thy skin, will unveil itself less black."

"Oh, I see," said Geeder. She was silent a moment. "I've been listening," she said. "I was standing there a long time."

"I thought you were the night traveller come to get me," Toeboy said. Timidly, he looked around, not quite certain of the shadows.

"For a moment there, I thought it had come to get us both," Uncle Ross said.

Geeder tried to smile but she was thinking and didn't have time to be amused at having frightened Toeboy and Uncle Ross.

"Maybe it's Zeely Tayber," she said. "Maybe she and the night traveller are the same thing." She blurted it out all at once.

"But she's not a slave or a prison man," Toeboy said.

Uncle Ross put his hand on Toeboy's shoulder and Toeboy was quiet. "Maybe it is," he said to Geeder. "Zeely Tayber comes every night with extra feed to check on the hogs."

"I don't think she has to come at all," Geeder said.

"No," said Uncle Ross.

"Then, why does she come?" Geeder asked.

"Well . . ." Uncle Ross said. He put away the cloth and the wax and prepared the table for the evening meal. The good smell of food cooking in the kitchen hung in the air, along with the careful sound of the last word he had said. Geeder waited.

"You could ask Zeely Tayber why she comes down the road," Uncle Ross said.

"She wouldn't talk to me," Geeder said. She re-

membered the hog run and the fact that Miss
Zeely hadn't said a word to her.

"She came by here in her own car just to see
you today," Uncle Ross said.

There was a stunned silence at the table. Geeder's unhappy expression changed to astonishment.
"The green coupe!" she said. "It was Miss Zeely!"

"What green coupe?" Toeboy said.

"Zeely Tayber has a little car," Uncle Ross said.
"She drove up here this afternoon just to see
Geeder. Geeder was out by the field, so she asked
me to give her a message."

Uncle Ross brought food from the kitchen. It
steamed up in the light but neither Geeder not
Toeboy touched any of it.

"What kind of message?" Geeder whispered at
last.

"Zeely asked that tomorrow you meet her at the
entrance to the catalpa forest. She wants to talk to
you," Uncle Ross said. "I think she's heard some
of the stories you've been telling about her."

Geeder sat quite still. She had expected something to happen. During the short time she had
slept upstairs, before she found Uncle Ross and
Toeboy talking, she had had the feeling of movement. Not dreaming, exactly, for she saw no pictures, but the feeling that there was something beyond her vision trying to catch up with her.

"Did she say whether Toeboy could come to the
meeting?" she asked Uncle Ross. She turned toward Toeboy but did not look at him.

"Zeely Tayber didn't mention Toeboy," Uncle Ross said. "She said she wanted to see you."

"I promised Bennie Green I would help work on his tree house," Toeboy said.

"I'll have to go by myself," said Geeder. The thought at once pleased and frightened her.

After they had eaten, and all night long, Geeder had a feeling that was a mixture of happiness and dread. She didn't sleep much because of it. By the following day, she was shaking with excitement. Her meeting was for two o'clock, but by one, she was ready to meet Miss Zeely.

Dressed for her meeting, Geeder wore shorts and a blouse with four strands of beads. One necklace was of painted and matched seeds from Haiti. The second consisted of large bloodstones and agates from India. The last two were selected from the glass beads she'd worn the night of the bonfire. Before leaving her room, Geeder looked closely at the photograph of the Watutsi woman.

"*Is* Zeely a queen?" she asked herself. "Did I make the whole thing up?"

The photograph was creased from handling but the form of the woman shone true as ever. Geeder took a deep breath. There wasn't any doubt in her mind that Zeely Tayber looked the same as the girl in the picture, and there wasn't any doubt that Zeely Tayber was a queen.

Geeder left the house at one thirty and walked toward the catalpa forest. The day was warm, with an unclouded, glazed sky. In the distance, there was haze, but around her, trees and road, bushes and fields, were crystal clear. The color of the catalpa trees was nearly black, with a tone of warm green somewhere deep within.

Geeder spoke out loud as she walked. "All the time with the hogs," she said, "she didn't once say anything, not a *word*. Who would have thought she'd want me to be with her now!"

Near the forest, an outgrowth of catalpas spread out on both sides of Leadback Road. They leaned high above Geeder, making a tunnel of branches and leaves. She entered the tunnel and the air turned cool. There was a hush of dampness and shade. The quiet of such great old trees made Geeder cautious, although they didn't frighten her. She respected the green worms on the leaves by keeping an eye on them as she walked. When she neared the entrance of the forest, she saw a green coupe parked close by the trees. At first, she hadn't seen it, for it was the exact color of the leaves. Standing in the entrance of the forest was Zeely Tayber. And Geeder, coming upon her all of a sudden, was shocked anew by her incredible height.

13

Geeder stood in amazement. Never had she seen Zeely dressed in such a way. She wore a length of varicolored silk wound around her delicate body and draped over her left shoulder. Around her head was a band of green silk, brilliant against her black hair. The long garment was beautiful and strange but the band around Zeely's hair was what held Geeder's attention. In her mind, she saw the picture of the Watutsi woman, the picture which right now she had hidden in her blouse. The Watutsi woman had worn such a headband.

"I'm glad you've come," Zeely said. Her voice was quiet, hardly above a whisper, and yet, it was perfectly clear. She smiled, adding, "Please follow me." She turned and led the way into the forest. Geeder, still unable to speak, followed.

Zeely plunged through stinging nettles. Often,

she stamped them down for Geeder or stopped to hold a bramble aside. At such times, Geeder forced herself to look up at Zeely; always, when she did so, she felt awfully small.

They stumbled into a clearing. Sprawling berry bushes grew in one dusty-green mesh that covered every foot of ground. Hedge trees surrounded the clearing in a perfect, enormous rectangle.

Geeder looked up at the sky. The sun beat down fiercely, almost blinding her. Now Zeely carefully inched through the bushes to the great shade trees bordering them.

"You must be careful," Zeely said, so suddenly she startled Geeder. "There may be caterpillars on the leaves. I believe they like to drop on people."

Bees and dragonflies moved and sung a monotonous humdrum. The smell of decay and life was so strong that Geeder felt unable to breathe. But the bad feeling passed by the time she and Zeely reached the border trees. They sat down under low branches. For a moment, there was a stir of wind high up in the leaves.

Geeder stared about at the berries which had grown ripe and then rotted and dried up on the bushes. "I didn't know all this was here," she said. "I don't know where we are."

"We are near the road," Zeely said, "but far away from where we entered."

They were silent for a time. Geeder didn't want to stare at Zeely so she played with her necklaces. When she grew tired of that, she picked long blades of grass to play with. By stretching the grass between her two thumbs, she created a fine instrument. She blew her breath against her thumbs; the blades vibrated. After a few tries, she was able to make two pure notes of sound. All the time she played this way, her mind raced with thoughts of Zeely. She was proud to be so near her again, proud and scared and unable to think of anything to say.

Zeely Tayber didn't seem to mind the silence between herself and Geeder. She was relaxed, serene. As she viewed Geeder from head to foot, her eyes were full of a strange light and dark.

Geeder sat across from Zeely. When Zelly began to stare at her hard, she became watchful and held herself more like a lady. She could not read Zeely's eyes, nor could she fathom why Zeely was looking at her that way.

What does she see? she wondered. What is it?

"Your many beads are pretty," Zeely said suddenly. "You have a lot of clothes?" She spoke as if Geeder were someone she had known for years. But her voice was halting, the way a person might speak when he hadn't had anyone to talk to for a long, long time.

Geeder was so startled by Zeely's question, her mind went empty. "Why, I don't know!" she said at last. "I've a dress to go to a party. I've got clothes for school. Mother buys them every fall and Christmas." She felt ashamed that she hadn't worn long pants instead of shorts to her meeting with Zeely.

"A girl should have clothes," Zeely said.

"Miss Zeely, I think your dress is about the most pretty one I've ever seen," Geeder said, shyly.

Zeely touched the bodice of her robe with her long fingers. Geeder could tell she was pleased by the compliment.

"I've had it a long time," Zeely said. "Twice a year, I hang it in the sun so that the colors will catch and hold the light." Very delicately, she gathered the skirt and smoothed it evenly about her feet. The colors leaped and glowed.

Geeder didn't know why they had started talking about clothes. Since they had begun to speak, she was bursting to ask Zeely about herself.

"Miss Zeely, do you come from Tallahassee?" she blurted out. "I think somebody told me you came from there."

"No," said Zeely, "we come from far to the north, from Canada."

"Canada!" Geeder said. The thought that Zeely came from such a place excited her. "I've never been there," she said. "Was it cold?"

"Where we were, it was cold," Zeely said. "It snowed and there was not much summer."

"Did you have hogs there, too?" Geeder asked. She entwined her fingers, eager to talk.

"We always have hogs," Zeely said. "We sell the best. We eat the meat of those that are left." She looked away from Geeder. "It's by them that we live."

The way Zeely spoke about the hogs made Geeder feel she had said something wrong. She grew uneasy. "Well," she said, "I just thought it was maybe Tallahassee you came from. I remember someone told me that."

"The same someone who says I am a queen?" Zeely asked. Her eyes held to Geeder's.

Geeder's hands flew to her face. "I didn't mean anything bad!" she cried. "Miss Zeely? Here!" She fumbled in her blouse and her hand shook as she gave Zeely the photograph of the Watutsi woman.

Zeely looked at the photograph. She smiled, vaguely, as though she didn't know she smiled. Finally, she gave the picture back to Geeder. She sat stiff and still. She could have been carved out of the trees, so dark was she seated there. Then, the rigid mask of her face melted, as if it were made of wax. A smile parted her lips. From deep in her throat came a warm, sweet giggle. She threw back her head and laughed and laughed. It was to Geeder a delicious, soft sound.

Geeder was so happy, she began to laugh, too, and got up to sit next to Zeely. All at once, they were side by side, just the way Geeder had dreamed it.

"You are very much the way I was at your age," Zeely said.

"You were like *me*?" Geeder said. "Were you just like me?"

Zeely smiled. "I mean that because you found this picture, you were able to make up a good story about me. I once made up a story about myself, too."

"Miss Zeely!" Geeder said. "I wouldn't have

told a soul if I hadn't found that picture. The picture is proof!"

Carefully, Zeely ran her long fingers over her robe. "My mother's people were Watutsi people out of Africa a long time ago," she said quietly.

"Just like the lady in the picture!" Geeder said.

"Yes," said Zeely, "and I believed that through my veins ran the blood of kings and queens! So it was that my mother came to make this robe for me," Zeely said. "I had asked her many questions about her people—I talked of nothing else for quite a while. She made this robe exactly like the ones they wore." Then she added, "I put it on today because wearing it, I can be more the way I was. You may touch it, if you like."

And very gently, Geeder touched it.

"It's just the most pretty thing," Geeder whispered, "it's the most pretty dress in the world!"

Zeely laughed. It was a quick, dry sound. Ever so slowly, the pleasure faded from her. A sadness came over her. Geeder sensed Zeely moving away to a place within herself.

"When I was your age," Zeely said, "my mother died."

"Oh!" Geeder said, "I'm awfully sorry, Miss Zeely."

Zeely didn't say anything for a time. Then, she began again. "I was tall," she said. "The children laughed at my skinny arms and my long legs. I wore my robe all the time, for I thought it beautiful and I wanted the children to believe about me what you have come to believe."

"But you *are* a Watutsi," Geeder said.

"Yes," said Zeely, "but wait . . ."

"You just said you came from Africa," Geeder said.

"Wait!" Zeely said. "We all came out of Africa—what of it?"

Geeder was quiet. She wasn't sure what was happening and she wished, suddenly, for Toeboy.

"I remember," Zeely began, "some time before my mother died, I wore my robe every day. My mother didn't like that. She would say, 'Zeely, you must wear clothes like other children, you must play and be like other children!' I would say, 'No, mama. No!' and one day she sat me down and told me a story."

"A story?" Geeder said.

"Yes," said Zeely. "One day, when my mother was very sick, she called me to her. She had this story to tell me. I remember she cautioned me to listen closely and I knew by the look in her eye that this was to be the tale I had always hoped for."

Zeely looked long and hard at Geeder. "It's an ancient tale, like these old trees around us. It means everything to me. Will you listen?"

Geeder said, "Yes, Miss Zeely, I will listen." She didn't understand all that Zeely had said. But she listened now, and waited, content for the time with the simple rise and fall of Zeely's soft voice.

14

Zeely Tayber told her story. Geeder listened, hardly breathing for fear she would miss some of it. Never had she heard such a tale. It was about the beginning of the world and it told of a young woman who waited for a message to come. The message would tell her who she was and what she was to do.

"In the beginning," Zeely said, "there were only a handful of people in each corner of the world. The Voice High Above had commanded them to wait for a message that would tell them their station in life. They were to sing while they waited so they could be found more easily. The Voice High Above had sent many couriers with messages. For each person, there were three couriers. The couriers for the young woman of my story were a gecko lizard, a coypu rodent from South America and a man whom The Voice High Above had not yet given a language to speak.

"The three couriers set out at once with their messages for the young woman," said Zeely. "The tiny gecko lizard's name was Ecko. He was nocturnal and travelled only at night. He had to sleep and hide from the light during the day, and he didn't make good time the first week of the search. The going became even harder for him when he left his country of Malaya. The climate changed too quickly for him to adjust to it. So it was that far from his home he died. His message for the young woman was buried forever beneath heavy snow."

"Miss Zeely, that's so sad!" Geeder said. "He should of known he couldn't make it!"

Zeely smiled but said no more about the gecko. She shifted her position so as to sit more comfortably and then continued her story.

"The coypu lived all his life in water," Zeely said. "His name was Coy and he did well the first week of the search. He swam through familiar rivers and lakes, stopping off to dine with relatives along his way. He was sure he would deliver his message in fine time.

"When Coy reached the edge of his continent, he swam swiftly to the Atlantic Ocean and began the hard part of his journey."

Geeder leaned forward, her hands folded tightly in her lap. She sensed by the change in Zeely's voice that something serious was about to happen.

"Coy headed south," said Zeely, "and used winds and currents for faster travel. But unknown to him, he was trapped in the powerful Brazil Current. He drifted northward and swam many days in chilly waters. One awful night, he was tossed about in the cold current of the Gibraltar Strait. He grew sick and feverish and was forced to seek shelter on the Rock of Gibraltar. After a short illness, he died from exposure. His message blew away with the wind," Zeely said, "never to be found." She lifted her hands above her head, held them there a second or two and then let them fall heavily into her lap.

Geeder understood the meaning of Zeely's hands in the empty air. She was silent, thinking of the poor coypu. It was a long time before Zeely resumed her story. When she did, the tone of her voice was full of suspense.

"We come now to the last courier," Zeely said. "He was the man and he had no name, for The Voice High Above had given him no name as yet, as He had given names to the animal men."

"What are animal men?" asked Geeder.

"Why, they are men the same as human men, except they are animals," said Zeely. Then she continued with her story.

"The man was confused by the time he completed the first week of travel. He couldn't find anyone to ask directions of. He had no language and could not talk to the animal beings, who spoke many tongues. Still, he travelled on, trying to somehow find his way.

"He was a man almost eight feet tall. Think of it!" Zeely said to Geeder. "He was that tall and he didn't know his height was unusual. There were no other people around to tell him. He was thin of limb, with skin as black as the darkest tree bark. Oh, he made a striking figure against the ice and snow!"

Zeely rocked from side to side as she said this, and Geeder could almost see the man walking in that cold place, a man black as night and tall as trees.

"The cold chilled the man to the bone," Zeely said. "Cold wind whipped at him, causing him to feel much pain. He was lonely, travelling so far by himself. It wasn't long before he realized that the country in which he found himself was not his own.

"One day, the man came upon an animal which had fallen on the sharp end of a broken sapling and died. The man tenderly took it in his arms and buried it beneath the snow. After this happened, there grew in his mind a picture of a long, wood shaft with a sharp point. At once, he set about making the shaft and fixed a sharp stone to its tip with strips of sapling bark. With the shaft, he could scrape a hole through the ice on any water he came upon and spear the fish beneath. This was how he was able to eat and survive. Then, many pictures grew in the man's mind. He began stalking a huge, white animal he had seen. The animal was a bear and he had seen it following him.

He had no fear of it, for he had no way of knowing it was hungry and a danger to him.

"As you see," Zeely said, "the man learned quickly. He took to hunting as though he had done such work all his life. He tricked the bear into falling down a deep trap he had dug. At the bottom of the trap were sharp poles which killed the bear when he fell on them.

"From the bear's fur, the man made a long cloak and warm shoes. He felt comfortable, then, and could travel more quickly. Many more cold weeks and months passed before he reached a place we know as Labrador. In front of him lay a mighty body of water. He was about to turn back—he knew nothing of swimming—when he heard a sweet, pure voice on a wind that was not cold."

"It's the girl!" Geeder said. "It's the girl he was supposed to find!"

"It *was* the young woman," said Zeely, "and the man recognized the wind as the wind of his homeland. He couldn't understand the voice because he had no language, but the wind was fresh with the scent of hills and grass.

"The man built a boat with sails made from the hides of animals," Zeely said. "He set out on the water, sailing with the wind, which grew warmer, and with the voice, that now taught him language. Soon, he threw away his cloak and shoes but was careful not to lose the message he carried in a pouch around his neck.

"One day," Zeely said, "the wind left him. He

drifted for months and months. He lived from fish of the water, birds of the air and sudden rains from the sky. Always, the voice was with him and always it told him not to be afraid.

"Early one morning the man awoke to find that he was in sight of land. He shouted his happiness and the voice at his ear laughed with pleasure. The land he saw was the coast of a continent; he landed at its northernmost port. Here, he found many peoples, for couriers had already delivered their messages. Mankind had begun to multiply.

"All kinds of people, seeing his great height, wondered if he were their king. They bowed to him and clung to him, begging him to lead them. He had no way of knowing what they spoke and turned sadly from them. He walked on and on until he came to a land oddly silent. There seemed to be no people anywhere, but something about the land felt comfortable. He stopped long enough to make himself a garment to wear, sandals for his feet and a staff to lean on. He walked many days in a wide valley and many nights through mountains. Often, he stood still and silent, looking down into this warm land he found so peaceful.

"One day," Zeely said, "the voice that was always with him seemed very close by. He looked down at his feet and on every side. At last, he looked up and there he found her, high above him on a green hill. Her figure against the deep blue sky was the most perfect image he had lived to see. Most pleasing of all to him was that she was as tall and dark as he.

"After such a long journey, the man had to climb the hill with his last strength. When he reached the young woman, he fell to his knees, trembling in every limb.

" 'Ho, traveller, welcome,' she said, 'I have waited years and years.'

" 'Ho, sister,' he answered slowly, for words didn't form quickly in his mind, 'I have travelled years and years and I have brought a message for you.'

"The man stood up then, bowed deeply and sat down. The young woman bowed and kneeled at his feet.

" 'You will please read the message,' she said, and this he read:

" *Young woman, you are of this man. You shall wed him, keep his house and bear his sons. You will trek many moons before you find people like yourselves. When you find them, you will join them and be good subjects to your king and queen.'* "

15

Geeder's thoughts had gone far, far away to the land of the courier and the young woman, to the green hill on which they first met and to the tribe of people they would have to search for. When Zeely stopped talking, Geeder sat waiting. Then, the clearing with its berry bushes came back to her in a rush of green and insect sound. She waited for Zeely to go on but Zeely did not.

"Is that all?" Geeder asked. "That's not the end of the story!"

"That's all," Zeely said, "and it's the truth as my mother told it to me."

"But I don't understand," Geeder said. "What's the truth?"

"My mother said she and I were descended from the girl the courier found."

Geeder sat quite still, with the photograph of

the Watutsi woman on her lap. She had held her hand pressed against it when Zeely first began her tale. Now, she smoothed her fingers over the photograph. "Oh, Miss Zeely," Geeder said, "I thought you were special even before I found the picture." It was as if she spoke to herself and not to Zeely.

Zeely stared at Geeder. "I asked you to come here because I wanted to tell you the tale my mother told," she said. "It means everything but you don't seem to care about it."

"Well, it really is a nice story," said Geeder. "I mean, I like it so much, with all that snow and that man and the girl." She clutched the photograph with both hands and then thrust it away to the ground. "But it's only a story. I came here today because . . . because *you* wanted me to! You wanted me to come to *be* with you, Miss Zeely!"

Zeely's eyes widened suddenly. Her long fingers covered her mouth in surprise. "Ahhh, now I see!" she said. "I did not realize that was why you came."

"You are the most different person I've ever met," Geeder said.

Zeely laughed softly. She drew her long legs up under her chin and folded her arms around them. In this way, she rocked slowly from side to side. Her eyes closed and there was a smile upon her lips.

Geeder watched her. All the time that Zeely had told her tale, she had sat stiff and tall in her long robe. Her shoulders had stood out sharply; her face had been all angles. Now, her features seemed to soften and flow into the deep shadows the trees made. Her hands and forearms were hidden in the long grass around her legs. Geeder looked at Zeely's black, black hair, dark as night, and it became a part of the darkening leaves above her head.

Geeder said, "It's you that comes down the road way late at night, isn't it, Miss Zeely?" She spoke into Zeely's ear.

Zeely nodded her head but did not open her eyes. "I come to look after my pigs," she said.

"And you carry a feed pail," said Geeder. "The moon going down slants onto it and it looks like it floats in the air. The moon is behind your back and so you don't have a face. It looks just like you don't have a head or any arms and you glide right above the ground."

"So," Zeely said, "you have seen me? I have seen you."

"You go by the house just before dawn," Geeder said. "You come early in the morning, anyhow. Why must you come so way late at night?"

"And why must you sleep there in the grass," Zeely asked, "so way late at night?"

"I like the stars," Geeder said, "and the moonshine."

"I like the night," said Zeely. She opened her eyes and stretched out her legs. Her shoulders drooped forward and her head fell back, slightly, as she studied the trees.

"Where I came from," Zeely said, "Canada, there was a lake.

"Oh, it was not a large lake," she said. "You could swim it, going slowly, in about fifteen minutes. I have done that. I have swum it when there was no moon or stars to light my way. Do you know what it is like to swim at night?"

"No," Geeder said, "I don't swim well, yet."

Zeely smiled, her eyes still in the trees. "It is like no other where," she said. "It is being in something that is all movement, that you cannot see, and it ceases to be wet. You must be very calm or you will not find your way out of it."

"Is that why you like the night?" asked Geeder.

"You see," Zeely said, looking at Geeder now, "the children wouldn't often swim in that lake, even in the daytime. A tiny old woman lived beside it. She wore a big bow in her hair that was very dirty. On top of the bow she wore a man's straw hat. She walked, bent forward, with a big cane for support. Often, she cackled to herself and pointed her cane at things. The children were afraid of her but I was not. Sometimes, I'd be swimming in the lake in the daytime, and she'd come upon me. 'Zeely Tayber,' she would call, 'I see you!' And I would call back to her, 'And I see *you*!' Then, she would call again. 'One of these times, I'll catch you!' she would say, and she would cackle and point her cane at me.

"Oh, no," Zeely said, "I was not afraid of her like the others were. I thought of her as a friend, almost. Then . . ."

"Then, what?" Geeder said.

Zeely looked away from Geeder. Her eyes turned inward upon themselves as Geeder had seen them do before.

"One night," Zeely said, "I had finished swimming and was pulling on my clothes when I heard footsteps on the path. I heard a cackle and I knew who it was. All at once, fear took hold of me. I had not ever thought of that little woman walking around at night, you see. At that moment, I was terrified. Quickly, I gathered my clothes and stood between a bush and tree, well hidden, I thought. And there she came along the path."

"Oh," said Geeder, softly. Her eyes were wide.

"She did nothing for a moment," Zeely said. "She stood there beside the lake looking at the dark water. Then, she looked around. She went up to a stone lying there beside her and touched it with her cane. It moved. It was a turtle and it scurried into the water."

"No!" said Geeder.

"Oh, yes," Zeely said. "And there was a fallen branch, twisted upon itself there, right next to the path. Vines grew over it. She poked one vine with her cane. It rippled. It was a snake and it slithered off into a bush near where I stood."

"No!" said Geeder.

"I couldn't believe my eyes," Zeely said, "I was so amazed by what I had seen."

"You must have been just scared to death!" Geeder said. She leaned against Zeely now, looking up at her, and Zeely leaned against Geeder.

Neither realized how close they had become, sitting there under the great trees.

"I was scared," Zeely said. "The woman kept cackling. Her back was turned to me. But I must have choked out loud on my fear, for suddenly she was silent. She spun around and stood there, facing the darkness where I was hidden.

" 'Zeely Tayber,' she said, 'I see you!' And I remember, I began to cry.

" 'Zeely Tayber,' she said again. She raised her cane right at me, and she was coming toward me. I could see her bow moving in the air. Suddenly, she had me by the arms. She was cackling again—I thought she would never stop.

"At last, she spoke," Zeely said. " 'Zeely Tayber,' she said, 'you have made a poor soul happy. You are the night and I have caught you!' "

"Oh!" said Geeder. "What a thing to happen!"

"Yes," said Zeely.

"What did you do?" asked Geeder.

"Do?" Zeely said. "I did nothing. Soon, the woman let me loose and went on her way, laughing and singing to herself. I was stunned by what she had said to me and I stood there in the darkness for many minutes. All at once in my mind everything was as clear as day. I liked the dark. I walked and swam in the dark and because of that, I was the *night!*

"Finally," Zeely said, "I told my mother about what had happened. My mother said that I simply had not known darkness well enough to tell the difference between a stone and a turtle and a vine and a snake. She said the snake and turtle had been there all the time. She said that since the woman was not quite right in her head, she had decided that I was the night because my skin was so dark."

"Did you believe what your mother said?" asked Geeder.

"I came to believe it," Zeely said. "I believe it now. But I was sorry my mother had said what she did. It meant I was only myself, that I was Zeely and no more."

Geeder sighed and looked down at her hands. "Things . . . are what they are, I guess," she said, quietly.

"Yes," said Zeely. "No pretty robe was able to make me more than what I was and no little woman could make me the night."

"But you *are* different," Geeder said. "You are the most different person I've ever talked to."

"Am I?" Zeely said, her voice kind. "And you want to be different, too?"

Geeder was suddenly shy. She took hold of her beads and ran her fingers quickly over them. "I'd like to be just like you, I guess, Miss Zeely," she said.

Zeely smiled. "To be so tall that wherever you went, people stared and questioned? You'd like to be able to call a hog to you and have it follow you as though it were a puppy?" She laughed. The sound of it was harsh. "Hogs see me as just another animal—did you know that? Their scent is my scent, that is all there is to it. As for being so tall, I would like once in a while not to have people notice me or wonder about my height. No," Zeely added, "I don't think you'd enjoy being like me or being different the way I am."

"I guess not, then," Geeder said. "I mean, I don't know." She stopped in confusion. She would never have imagined that Zeely didn't like being tall. "I want to be . . . to be . . ." She paused.

"Whoever it is you are when you're not being Geeder," Zeely said, finishing for her. "The person you are when you're not making up stories. Not Geeder and not even me, but yourself—is that what you want, Elizabeth?" Zeely looked deeply at Geeder, as if the image of her were fading away. "I stopped making up tales a long time ago," she said, "and now I am myself."

Geeder was so startled she could not say anything. And the way Zeely called her Elizabeth, just as though they were the same age, caused a pleasant, quiet feeling to grow within her. What she had promised herself at the beginning of the summer crossed Geeder's mind. *I won't be silly. I won't play silly games with silly girls.*

But I *was* silly, she thought. I made up myself as Geeder and I made up Zeely to be a queen.

She let go of her bright necklaces and smoothed her hands over her hair.

"Myself . . ." she whispered. "Yes, I guess so."

Zeely Tayber ruffled the creases from her long robe and then stood up to leave. She was tall and beautiful there, before Geeder. Her expression was soft.

"I want to thank you, Geeder," she said, "for

helping me with the sow last Saturday. I don't know how much you know about hogs, but they are miserable creatures. My father is tired of them and so am I. I take care of them as much as I can, to see they are treated well. It is hard work and I don't have much time for friends."

She touched Geeder lightly on the hair. Her long fingers fluttered there a moment, as lithe as the wings of a butterfly, before they were gone. Zeely knew before Geeder did that Geeder was close to tears.

"You have a most fine way of dreaming," Zeely said. "Hold on to that. But remember the turtle, remember the snake. I always have."

Geeder didn't see Zeely leave the clearing. The colors of bush and tree swam in her eyes and Zeely melted away with them.

16

Geeder sat under the catalpa trees until the sky was streaked with light of the setting sun. She got up, chilled. Her legs felt cramped and there was a dull, uncomfortable feeling in the pit of her stomach. When she came out of the forest onto the road, she found the tunnel the catalpa trees made dark as night.

"I don't mind the dark of it," she whispered. "It's being alone in it that's the trouble." She walked quickly through the tunnel, full of sadness.

Toeboy waited for Geeder behind Uncle Ross' hedge. He had waited all afternoon and was beginning to worry, when he heard Geeder on the road. He jumped up when she entered the yard.

"I don't want to talk right now," Geeder said. She did not even glance at him. "I'm going up to rest awhile before dinner."

Toeboy was too surprised to say anything. He wanted to know right away what Zeely had said; yet, he was stopped by the new tone in Geeder's voice. He needed no one to tell him that she was awfully upset about something. He went away quietly to tell Uncle Ross of her return.

Uncle Ross and Toeboy were eating by the time Geeder came down to supper. If a stranger had seen her go up, he wouldn't have believed she was the same girl who now came down.

"Geeder!" Toeboy said, "Just look at you!"

For the first time this summer, Geeder had come to dinner wearing a dress. It was a nice dress. Toeboy had to admit that. It was yellow with pretty white flowers. In her hair, Geeder wore a white ribbon. Toeboy couldn't help laughing at the ribbon and Geeder grew angry. Still, she didn't yell at him. In fact, she nodded politely and sat down next to him.

"You look the way you do when we go to school," Toeboy said to her. "You don't look like Geeder at all."

"Well, Elizabeth," Uncle Ross said, "you've been gone a good part of the day."

Toeboy stared at Uncle Ross. He had called Geeder Elizabeth. Toeboy felt like saying that there sat Geeder and not Elizabeth. But when he looked at Geeder, he couldn't say a word. There was no doubt at all that right beside him was Elizabeth.

"Uncle Ross, I didn't mean to stay away so

long," Geeder said, "but Miss Zeely Tayber had so much to tell me . . ."

"Geeder, was she mad?" Toeboy wanted to know.

"No, she wasn't mad," Geeder said. "She wasn't what I had expected at all."

"What *had* you expected?" Uncle Ross asked.

"I wanted her to say right away that she was a queen," Geeder said.

"Didn't she look like a queen up close?" Toeboy asked.

"I'd better tell you," Geeder said. She pushed her plate away. "If I don't tell you as fast as I can, I won't believe it ever happened."

Geeder told Toeboy and Uncle Ross just the way Zeely had been and she didn't change anything at all. She told them about the robe Zeely had worn and every detail of their meeting. She described the clearing for Toeboy, saying how frightened she had been, seated so close to Zeely. At last she told them about Canada and about the little old woman. She told them the long story of the three couriers. When she had finished, Uncle Ross sighed and smiled.

"When you stayed away so long," Toeboy said, "I thought for sure you must have found out Zeely Tayber was a queen." He leaned on his hand, staring thoughtfully into space.

Geeder looked at Toeboy and then at Uncle Ross. She smoothed her hands over her dress and patted her dark curls.

"It's true," she said, simply. "There's not another thing in the world Zeely Tayber could be but a queen."

Both Toeboy and Uncle Ross were taken by surprise. Before either one could say anything, Geeder was talking. —

"Listen!" she said, almost whispering, so that Uncle Ross and Toeboy had to lean forward to hear. Her hands rose before her. She began to divide and shape the air, as though she were making images out of nothing.

"I don't mean queen like you read in books or hear on the radio, with kingdoms and servants and diamonds and gold! I mean queen when you think how Miss Zeely *is*. Listen! All these hogs going down the road and into town, smelling up the town and squealing. Nat Tayber all covered with mud, just cruel and mean, worse than any animal—I don't care if he is Zeely's father. But did anyone ever think of Miss Zeely as smelling like those hogs or being anything other than kind! And listen! All those animals being dirty—no, filthy! Covered with flies and hog wallow, with a stench you couldn't get rid of in a hundred years. But would you think Miss Zeely was anything but a lady? I mean, working with hogs, having to feed them and walk through them and handle the babies! And having to stay close to old Nat all the time because he is her father and because he gets mean with the hogs sometimes. She doesn't even know that folks talk about her behind her back. She wouldn't ever think folks could be as silly as to think she had bewitched those animals. She does her work and I bet she does it better than anybody could.

"Because," Geeder said, and then she paused a moment, "it's not what a person stoops to do—oh, no, it's not! It's what's inside you when you dare swim in a dark lake with nobody to help if something should happen. Or, when you walk down a dark road way late at night, night after night.

"Oh, she's a queen," Geeder said, "Miss Zeely is the best kind you'd ever want to see!"

There was a silence at the table. They could hear the sound of crickets through the window screen. Uncle Ross looked out the window, surprised to find that night had fallen. He picked up his knife and fork. He had placed them beside his plate when Geeder had first begun to talk about Zeely Tayber.

They finished eating. There was not much talking. After supper, Toeboy and Uncle Ross went into the living room. Geeder went up to her own room. There, she pulled one of the cherry-wood chairs up close to the window. She sat down, gazing out into the night and the west field and stars beyond.

"So much to see here," she whispered. "Just a few days and nights left before we go back home. Where's the summer melted to? I don't recall it going.

"That's because of Miss Zeely," she said. "She was the days and nights put together."

Geeder stared at the stars. They resemble people, she thought. Some stars were no more than bright arcs in the sky as they burned out. But other stars lived on and on. There was a blue star in the sky south of Hesperus, the evening star. She thought of naming it Miss Zeely Tayber. There it would be in Uncle Ross' sky forever.

"Will I come here again?" she whispered. "Will I come back to see her? No. What's to see? If I do come again, it'll be to remember the nights at the same time I'm living them. If she's here, I will see her. But it will be all right if she's gone off to some other place. There will be that star."

Geeder was an hour or more at the window before at last she moved away. She turned on the light and placed the chair where it belonged. She walked around the room collecting all her necklaces from the backs of the two chairs, from the bedposts and from the dresser-drawer knobs. When she had them all, she placed them in the box at the bottom of her suitcase. There they shone in bright flashes.

She looked up, startled. Her hands were still in the suitcase touching the bright necklaces as she looked slowly around the room.

"Did I take it back?" she said. "Where's the flashlight?" Her hands jerked away from the necklaces. "The night traveller!" she whispered. "But no," she said, "it was Miss Zeely all the time."

Geeder found the flashlight behind the window curtains. She placed it on her bureau so she would remember to return it to Uncle Ross. Then, she sat down on the bed and picked up two of her glass-bead necklaces. She swung them before her, like pendulums.

"Remember the turtle," she murmured, "remember the snake."

She swung the beads back and forth until she grew dizzy from watching the changing light of them. She was hungry again, as she usually was soon after supper. Maybe Uncle Ross had saved her a sweet potato.

"I only had one," she said. "I was talking so much, I didn't even taste it."

The MS
READ-a-thon needs
young readers!

Boys and girls between 6 and 14 can join the MS READ-a-thon and help find a cure for Multiple Sclerosis by reading books. And they get two rewards — the enjoyment of reading, and the great feeling that comes from helping others.

Parents and educators: For complete information call your local MS chapter, or call toll-free (800) 243-6000. Or mail the coupon below.

Kids can help, too!